When A Thug
Finds True Love

By

Jazmine Wright

Legal Notes

Copyright © 2016

Published By Major Ink Publications

www.majorinkpublications.com

ALL RIGHTS RESERVED.

Dedication

I dedicate my first book to my kids, family, friends and everyone who supported me along the way. Thanks for all the encouragement and for pushing me when I wanted to give up so many times, you know who you are. I also want to thank everyone who said I couldn't do it. Because of you, I stayed motivated and pushed myself harder. Guess what, I did it!

CHAPTER 1

EGYPT

I'm Egypt Parker, and my twin sister's name is Paris. Around our hood, we're known as the Parker twins. We grew up in Camden, New Jersey and still live here with our mother, Nadine— that's if you can even really call her a mother. After our father died, she pretty much stopped being a real mother to us. She turned to crack cocaine as a means to cope with the pain and devastation she felt over losing my father. That was when our entire world changed.

No one can begin to imagine the shit that Nadine put us through. We have lived in just about every neighborhood in New Jersey. She would do well for a couple of months, but then she would fall right back into her crack habit. She would stop paying the bills, and we would end up right back on the streets. I changed schools so much that my grades fell way behind. It got to the point where I barely went to school at all. I had to stay at home and take care of my momma. When she couldn't get her hands on any crack, she went through her detox stage. It was way more than I could handle, so I ended up dropping out a few months ago. I haven't told my momma yet because I plan on going back as soon as possible. I just hate to be so far behind everyone else, but I just don't have the time right now. I'm only 16, and it's like the weight of the world is on my shoulders. I swear, Nadine is the worst parent I know, but I hold onto the memories of the kind of mother she was before my father died.

My father was a police officer for ten years before he was killed in the line of duty by a drunk driver. Paris and I were only nine years old at the time, and it crushed my soul to pieces. That's the last time I can remember my momma being normal. There's not a day that goes by that I don't wish he was still here. I know our life would be entirely different. We would still have our house instead of living in the projects. I would still have my mother instead of this empty, cold, heartless woman.

I often try to block out many of the things that my mother has allowed, but sometimes the memories still seep through. One of the memories that I can never seem to block out is my mother pimping me out for drugs. I have flashbacks of my initial fear, the smell of their skin, and how I eventually became numb, but I never let any of them touch Paris. I vowed to protect her with my life. I made Paris hide in the closet every time those old nasty ass perverts came into our room. They were so high half of the time that they didn't know the difference anyway. I hated to hear her crying for me as I screamed over and over again for someone to come and rescue me. I cried for my daddy. I cried for my best friend, Rodney, but no one ever came. I just dealt with the abuse the best that I could. Whenever they were inside of me, I would often think of Rodney. My thoughts would drift to wondering where life had taken him after all these years. Had he gotten married or had any kids yet? Sometimes, I'd go so far as to imagine it was Rodney inside of me instead of those ol' nasty bastards.

Rodney is the only male outside of my daddy that I knew always had my back. We grew up together back in the day. His dad and my dad were good friends. Rodney's dad raised him as a single parent, so my parents helped him out whenever they could. My mom was the head warden for the local women's prison at the time, and she would let Rodney catch a ride with us to school every morning. We were neighbors for a long time, until we started bouncing around from place to place. No matter where we moved, Rodney would always come visit until he and his father moved away to Virginia. I always wished that I could have gone with them. It broke my heart to see them leave. I knew there was no way in hell my momma was gonna let me go, so I didn't even ask. I swear that was the saddest day of my life outside of losing my daddy. I remember the last day I saw him like it was yesterday. I was in the 9th grade, and I had just gotten my tonsils taken out. I couldn't go to school for a whole week, and Rodney had agreed to help me with my missing assignments so that I wouldn't fall behind. Even though he was in the 11th grade, he still stopped by all my classes to get my homework. Our school had early dismissal on Wednesdays, so Rodney decided to come by that afternoon to drop my school work off. My momma was out and Paris was staying late for band practice, so I had the house all to myself. I texted Rodney and told him that I had left the back door unlocked just in case I wasn't out of the shower by the time he got there. I stepped out of the shower and dashed across the hall to my bedroom to dry off and change. Surprisingly, Rodney was already waiting for me in my bedroom instead of the living room, like usual. I almost lost my breath as soon as I saw him sitting at the foot of my bed. He hadn't even noticed me at first until I screamed.

"Aaaaaaaggghhh!"

There I was standing in the doorway, naked as the day I was born. I ran out the room to go get the towel I had left in the bathroom. I was so embarrassed.

"What's wrong with you, girl? Damn, chill out!"

"Go away! What are you doing in my room? I thought you was going to wait for me in the living room!" I yelled through the bathroom door.

"Well, since you wasn't feeling good, I thought you would be in bed. I figured that's why you texted and said you left the door unlocked. I thought you didn't want to have to get up."

"I – I wanted to freshen up a little. I thought you were gonna wait downstairs," I stuttered.

"Eeeewwwhhh! Stank ass! Yeah, I think you might have needed that. Smells like a good idea. What you been doing up in this room anyway?" Rodney joked.

"Shut up, boy! You so stupid. You know I'm sick and don't

feel good right now, so leave me alone and go away so I can get dressed, please!"

"Why? You scared to get dressed in front of me? It ain't like I've never seen you naked before. Right?"

"Hush, we're not kids anymore! I don't want you looking at me   like   that!"   I   yelled. "Ugggh, you get on my nerves! Can you please go downstairs so I can get dressed?"

"Come on out here, girl. It ain't like you the first chick I saw in a towel. Damn!"

"Yeah, I'm sure I'm not!" I said as I opened the door and proceeded to my bedroom. I guess Rodney picked up on my attitude, so he reached out and grabbed me by the arm. He already knew I had a crush on his sexy chocolate ass ever since we were kids. He was a couple years older than me, but it still didn't change the way I felt about him. I knew my crush was mutual, even though we were only kids.

"So, you're just gonna walk right by me like that?"

"Yep! Sure is."

"Stop playing, E! You gonna show me what's under that towel again or what?" Rodney whispered in my ear; he then took his tongue and licked down my neck. My body shook as he took my earlobe into his mouth and started sucking on it.

"Umm, you better stop. Your girl ain't gonna like that."

"What you talking about, girl? I don't have a girl. I have friends, and there's a difference. Plus, I can't help it if you taste so good."

"Whatever, Rodney! Get off of me so I can get dressed, please," I said, pushing him aside as I walked into my room.

"That's how you're gonna do me? You're just gonna push my away like that, huh?"

"I don't have time for your games, Rodney. You're the biggest dog I know. All you want is ass. I see you with a different girl every other day. You must think I'm stupid."

I already knew Rodney's lying ass couldn't be faithful to just one female; yes, I did like him, but I wasn't going to share him with anyone. He knew that he could come to me whenever he decided to stop running after every big butt he saw walking by.

"Yeah, but you're different. I want more from you."

"Umm huh, I bet so. More like what?"

"I just want more. I know you younger than me and still living at home with ya moms, but you know what I do in these streets, E. You know it's not a game. You know I can give you whatever you want if you let me. Just not right now. I know what you and Paris are going through. Trust me. I understand, but you also know momma Nadine will have my ass thrown under the jail house if I take you away from here."

I thought long and hard about the things Rodney would say to me. I knew he was making a name for himself in the streets with the old heads. All of his promises did sound good, and I wanted to escape the pain that I was enduring at home, but I couldn't leave Paris behind. I quickly shook the thought from my head.

"I just don't know about you, Rodney. You do have a way with words, and I need to leave this house fast. I can't keep living like this."

"Come here and forget about that for a minute. Here, touch it. You know you want to feel daddy. See how happy you got him?" Rodney said as he grabbed my hand and placed it in the front of his jeans by the zipper. I rubbed my hand across the huge bulge that was sticking out.

Thanks to Nadine, I lost my virginity a long time ago. I already knew what was about to happen next. The difference was that this was with someone I cared about. I'd never had sex with a guy that I actually had feelings for until that moment. Rodney must have felt how my body tensed up because he whispered in my ear for me to calm down.

"Stop, Rodney. We shouldn't be doing this. I don't think it's a good idea. What if someone catches us?"

"Chill out Egypt, damn. Why you acting all nervous and shit? What the fuck you scared of?"

"I'm not scared!"

"Come here and sit next to me."

I did as he asked and took a seat beside him on the edge of my bed. My eyes were focused on the floor.

"Look E, you don't have to be afraid or ashamed, aight? It's against the law what those men did to you. Your mother is the one who should be embarrassed. Trust me, I'll never hurt you like they did."

"It's not just that. I don't want you thinking I'm that kind of girl."

"What kinda girl?"

"The easy kind. The one that gives it up fast with no questions asked. Plus, I don't want to jeopardize our friendship just for one night of fun. We're still young, and I'm not sure if I'm ready to lose my friend if something goes wrong. On top of that, you've got a girlfriend whether you want to admit it or not."

"I respect that. I understand what you're saying, but you know I've always liked you. Haven't I always told you that you're the girl? That I'm gonna marry you one day? Plus, that girl and I are just friends and you know it. It's not my fault them hoes be trying to claim a nigga. I'm single, so I do what I want."

"Whatever. We were just kids back then, and I'm pretty sure you said a lot of things to a lot of different girls. So, do you just go around and fuck all your friends?"

"Here we go with this shit…no Egypt, just forget it. You know damn well what I meant. Never mind, and here's your homework. I got to bounce. I got stuff to do. You over here trippin' for no reason," Rodney said, pulling the wad of papers out of his back pack and tossing it on the bed.

"I'm not trippin', Rodney. You just don't understand. You think everything is supposed to go your way all the time."

"I understand a lot, but I don't have time for your drama today. I got money to make."

"Well, go make it then!"

"Man, I'll holla at you later. I don't know what your problem is today, but I'm out," Rodney said as he started walking toward the door. I stopped him by pulling his book bag.

"What now? You wanted me to come drop your papers off, so I did."

"Well, you don't have to be so nasty about it."

"I'm not. Shit, I'm just saying…you're acting all crazy. Ain't nobody got time for all that."

"So, why are you snapping at me all of a sudden. As soon as I didn't want to have sex, your attitude changed. You weren't acting like that a few minutes ago. You couldn't keep your hands off me. Now, you've suddenly got paper to make."

"What do you want me to do E, huh? You know my lifestyle, and you of all people know what I'm dealing with deep inside. I want you more than anything, but you and I both know I'm not the right guy for you. Hell, I'm not right for anybody right now. You're way different than the type of females I'm used to dealing with. You're a good girl. You're not like some of these hood chicks I see out in the streets every day. These hoes are just looking for some good dick and a little bread to get their hair and nails done. At this moment, that's all I'm willing to offer. I want you more than anyone in the whole world, but I know I can't have you. I don't want to ruin your life, but at the same time, I think that's why I want you more every time I see you. We play it cool in front of everybody, but we both know the truth. You may never admit it, but I know deep down you feel the same way I do."

I just stood there silently listening to every word Rodney said. He was completely right about everything. I had been in love with him since I was eight-years-old. He had even proposed to me with a bag of gummy worms, which was my favorite candy. We promised each other that if we ever got married that it would be to each other. I couldn't believe he remembered that because I had almost forgotten about our little pact.

"Yes, I know what kinda lifestyle you live, and I also know what comes with it. That's what scares me."

"Don't be afraid. You know I would never let anything happen to you," Rodney said as he kissed me on the lips. It felt so good. His lips were so soft.

We kissed for what seemed like an eternity. I was still naked, so he started massaging my breasts. I loved the way his hands felt on my body. He laid me back on the bed as we continued to kiss. He put his hand between my legs and started rubbing me softly, then he released my tongue and used his to travel from my neck down to my navel. Once he reached my sweet spot, he placed gentle kisses all over it. I moaned from the way his tongue was dancing around on my love button. My body jerked over and over like I was having a seizure until I exploded on his face. He didn't slow down at all. He just kept sucking and licking. I thought I was going to lose my mind when I felt his finger slide inside of me while he was still using his tongue as a weapon against my pool of moisture. I couldn't take it anymore. I tried to scoot back from his grip, but he held me tighter. I moaned over and over until he finally had mercy on me. He moved his kisses back to my breasts. He placed my right hand on his belt buckle to unfasten it. I began to unzip his zipper as he pulled his shirt over his head, and then tossed it onto the nightstand. His pants fell to the floor, and he was standing there in nothing but his red boxer shorts. I couldn't believe my eyes. His magic stick was so huge. He reached into his jeans and pulled out a condom in a gold wrapper. He ripped the pack open and slowly rolled the rubber up over his huge dick. Once it was on, he slid his finger inside my wetness for a few minutes, then pushed his hard rod inside of me.

"Ummmm, Rodney it feels so good. Yes!"

"Yeah, you like that? You want me to stop?"

"Yes," I moaned, loving the way he felt. "Mmm, I like it. No, please don't stop."

"Ummm baby, I won't stop. Shit, it feels so good!"

We did it all afternoon, and it was magical. The time flew by so fast. Rodney's phone kept ringing and I knew my momma would be coming home soon, so we decided to end our day. I would have never let him go if I had known that would be the last time I would see him. He left without even saying goodbye. It was like they packed up and moved during the middle of the night. We weren't neighbors anymore, but we still went to the same school. Rodney also hung out in our apartment complex every day to hustle. It was like one day he was in the hood, and then the next day he had vanished into thin air.

CHAPTER 2

EGYPT

After Rodney and his dad moved, things were tougher for me and Paris. Sometimes, I had to beg and borrow so Paris and I could eat. Thank God for Ari. She had her own spot and got food stamps for her daughter, Kiki. She made sure Paris and I ate every night. Outside of Rodney and my twin sister Paris, Ari was my best friend in the whole wide world. The three of us have been tight since I was about 12 years old. Ari was only 18 now and had the perfect body. She looked way more mature than her age, though. Some people gained weight when they had a baby, but it filled Ari out in all the right places. She had to drop out of school before graduating in order to take care of her newborn daughter, Kierra. We called her 'Kiki' for short, and she was the sweetest baby ever. I hated that Ari was stuck being a single mom. Kiki's father was killed when Ari was only three months pregnant. That left her all alone to raise a newborn. I didn't have much, but I did what I could for the both of them, even if my life depended on it. I knew she would do the same for me. Paris and I babysat for her whenever we could, but since I hadn't been going to school lately, I kept her for Ari during the day. I could hide out from my momma too.

"Make sure you pack more than two bottles this time, girl. You know this little girl got a big ass appetite. You remember what happened last time, right?" I asked, leaning over and pinching baby Kiki on her chubby little cheek as she giggled and kicked her tiny legs around in the air.

"Ugh! Don't remind me. I was thinking the same thing. Dang, stay out of my head, E."

"Well, you know what they say, right? Great minds think alike."

"Whatever girl, but aye, I want to ask you something."

"What?"

"I need you to watch the baby until Sunday for me. Please say you're free!"

"Ari, you know I don't mind helping you out whenever I can, but you know how my mama be trippin', girl. You think I want to hear her go on and on for hours? You know my momma crazy as hell."

"Come on, E. Please, please. It's only two days, Egypt. I'll be back first thing Sunday morning, I promise. You can stay over here," Ari begged.

"I don't feel like hearing my momma mouth today. You know she ain't bout to let me stay over here the whole weekend. Damn, I thought you only wanted me to watch her for a couple of hours. Why can't your grandma keep her while you're gone?"

"Because she got to work a double shift at the hotel this weekend. Trust me, I asked her already. You know how my family is, girl. They ain't trying to help me."

"Um huh, yeah right, I hear you. So, where are you going for you to have to be gone for two damn days?"

"Ugggh! None of your business, nosey. Always trying to see what I got going on. I'll tell you when I get back. So, are you gonna keep her? You know if it wasn't important, I wouldn't be begging you."

"Whatever heifer, don't make me slap you, and I guess so. But if I get cussed out because of you, it's gonna be trouble when you get back here."

"Ha ha, yea right. You so crazy, girl."

"I'm so serious, but aye, you know what I was thinking about the other day?"

"No, what's that?"

"I was sitting in the park just thinking we should pack all our stuff up and just run away. You remember back in the day? How we used to always say one day we were gonna run away from here where nobody could find us?"

"Ha! Ha! Ha! Yeah, I remember. That was a long time ago, girl. I think that we was about what…12 years old, right?"

"Yea, something like that! Ugh, girl I'm so ready to leave this dead ass town. One day, I'm gonna leave. Just watch and see. I wish I knew where my homeboy Rodney moved to, 'cause I would be right there. My momma can't stop me from leaving now."

"Whatever girl, we stuck here. Look around, sweetheart; this is life, the only life we will ever know, so you might as well get used to it."

I looked around the room and saw how the rats and roaches were walking around as if they owned the place. I listened as the hustlers in the hallway shot dice and sold their crack right outside the door like it was nothing. The projects I lived in were even worse.

"No, I refuse to live like this forever! This will not be my life, and Camden, New Jersey will not be my home. You can mark my words."

"Okay E, whatever! You just keep that dream alive, and I'ma keep packing Kiki's stuff," Ari replied sarcastically, as she walked through the small one-bedroom apartment throwing things inside the red and white diaper bag.

"Put enough diapers in there too. You know how you are. It ain't like I got no money to be buying no more."

"Hush, and put her sandals on, please. Dang, always talking shit! You act like I'm crazy or something. It ain't like this is the first time she done spent the night away from home, you know."

"You are crazy. It's not my fault. Now hurry up 'cause you're starting to get on my nerves."

"Shut up, and get the sandals out of the closet and put them on her before Peanut's crazy ass gets here. Can you do that? You know his ass stay in a rush."

I never asked Peanut for money because I didn't want him thinking I owed him any more than I already did. He could be a good guy when he wanted to, but he could be a monster at times also. He told me that he loved me, but I knew he really didn't. He thought that just because I was young that I was naïve. Little did he know, I was smarter than he thought. I had a plan—one that didn't involve him or my momma.

"Nope! Isn't that your job?"

"Girl, go get the damn shoes. You always got to be a smart ass."

"Yep, I sure do," I said, playfully waving the sandals in front of her face.

"Move. Ugh, you play too much. Dang!" snapped Ari, slapping the shoes out of her face.

The sound of a horn honking outside the bedroom window made both Ari and I jump.

"Oh, that's just Peanut. I forgot that he was driving Aunt

Dee's truck while his car is in the shop getting a new paint job," Ari said, peeking through the ruffled up blinds.

"Um huh, I figured that was his crazy ass out there blowing the horn like he ain't got no damn sense," I said.

Ari quickly gathered all the baby's things up and threw the diaper bag over her shoulder, laughing as she followed me outside. She handed the diaper bag to me as she opened the back door of the all-white Escalade that belonged to their aunt.

"Hey. Was sup, cousin?"

"Cooling, what you been up to, Ari? I ain't seen your ass in a minute."

"Ain't shit. I've been out all day looking or a job. Ugh, I hate dealing with them damn white folk. They be acting like you owe them something. I swear that shit irked my nerves. They look at you like you're crazy and shit."

"Ha ha girl, you so damn wild. What's good, E; you can't speak?"

"Wassup bae, I was about to but y'all was talking," I said, leaning over to kiss him on the lips, but he turned away.

"You better stop all that in front of Kiki."

"You a mess, boo. It ain't like she knows what's going on, but hold on a sec, I need to tell Ari something really quick. I'll be right back."

I walked over and stood on the sidewalk to talk to Ari for a few minutes. That was until Kiki started whining with her spoiled ass.

"Yo E, let's go! I got moves to make and y'all know Kiki don't like sitting still for a long time," Peanut yelled through the cracked window.

Ari and I hugged and said our goodbyes, then I hopped inside the truck and fastened the seat belt around my waist. As soon as I sat down in the truck, Peanut looked over at me and turned his nose up in disgust. I already knew his ass was mad at me for being over at Ari's house. They were first cousins, but he hated for me to be around her because of the reputation she has around the hood. That's not the real reason, though. Peanut's ass was just jealous and taking it out on me for some reason.

Hell, I got my own mind and whatever Ari does has nothing to do with me, I thought to myself as I adjusted the seatbelt. Peanut reached over and turned the radio up, and then sped off down the block.

CHAPTER 3

PEANUT

Egypt was the most beautiful girl that I'd ever laid eyes on. I mean, she was truly the definition of a natural beauty. She stood at 5'3 with a caramel complexion and bangin' ass body. She had curves on top of curves, and her skin tone was so damn sexy and smooth without a scar in sight. I could get lost inside of those sexy brown eyes of hers. She was the kind of girl I would take home to meet my mama—if she'd learn to act right and control that smart ass mouth. I didn't know what it was about her. At times, she made me feel like she was the only girl in the world for me. At other times, she made me want to break her fuckin' neck.

I reached over and turned the volume down on the radio as I cut my eyes over at Egypt. She was sitting over there like her ass didn't have a care in the world. I drove in silence for about five more minutes before I decided to talk to her.

"So, why you ain't been answering my calls all day? I been blowin' your silly ass up ever since I woke up. All I've been getting is the damn voice mail. What's up with that shit?"

"Um-mm I-I was watching Kiki all day for Ari," stuttered Egypt.

"What the hell does that have to do with your phone? I pay the damn bill, but I can't get through to your ass? Bitch, you got shit twisted if you think you're gonna play me. You probably been with one of them little niggas out there. I know about all them fucking dudes Ari little hoein' ass be having at her crib. You think I'm stupid or something? Yeah, that's it. You think I love having my bitch in niggas' faces all day, huh?"

"Calm down, Peanut. Ain't nobody trying to play you! The damn phone was turned off while it was charging," I snapped.

"Who you think you gettin' loud with? Don't make me slap your silly ass. I know damn well you ain't been charging your phone up all day. So you can sell that bullshit to somebody else."

"Whatever Pe-"

Wham!

"Aggghhhhh!" Egypt screamed.

*****

EGYPT

The slap was so loud that Kiki started crying. It was like she felt my pain. Peanut was 18, which made him two years older than me. We'd been dating for a year now. I didn't know how we managed to stay together that long. I just knew that as soon as I got a job, I was leaving this fucked up ass life behind me. At one time, I thought he really loved me, but now I've gotten used to the abuse from Peanut. It was no different than what my mom let happen to me. It made me hate love. There was no such thing as love. Only Paris and Ari loved me. Anyone else who ever spoke those words to me either ended up leaving me, like Rodney did, or hurting me. I was leaving it all behind. I couldn't take it anymore. Life wasn't supposed to feel like this.

"Where are you, Rodney?" I whispered to myself. I thought Peanut had heard me because he looked at me strange as soon as I said it. *Oh well, I don't care if he did hear me. At least it's the truth*, I thought as I stared out the window, holding my hand over the side of my face where Peanut had just smacked the hell out of me.

Peanut was 5'9. He was tall, chocolate, and sexy as hell. He reminded me of the R&B singer Tyrese, except he rocked his hair short with waves. He dressed like the pretty boy type in khakis, polo shirts, and Sperry's. He was definitely a ladies' man, and the bitches loved his swag. No matter where we went, there was always some little hood chick up in his face. I stayed having to fight over his cheating, lying, no-good ass. I didn't know why I even stayed with him. I guess mainly because he wouldn't let me leave. He found me every time I tried to run away. I had tried to leave him so many times, only to be beaten the entire way back home. There was no use, so I just stayed and took it, but I was tired now. I didn't want to live like this. Where was my happy ever after?

*****

PEANUT

"Stop all that crying, bitch! You should learn to keep your fuckin' mouth closed and you won't get hit in it."

I hated having to put my hands on Egypt. It's like she didn't understand that I really loved her stubborn ass. She just pushed my buttons sometimes. She knew just what to do to make me mad. Even though she knew damn well that I didn't play when it came to her ass. I wanted to know where she was at all times. She knew this, but she continued to test me.

Her ass would learn to respect me one way or the fucking other. She better realize I'm nothing to play with, or I'll beat it into her dumb ass. Every bitch in the hood wanted to be in her position. They all wanted to be down on a nigga's team just to see what was in my pockets, but that would never happen. I ain't have shit for their asses, but this "D". I knew E was young and knew nothing about life yet, but I was going to mold her into the woman I wanted her to be. I was the one who taught her everything she knew, even down to cooking and cleaning. I even taught her how to take care of her personal hygiene, unlike that crack head hoe she called momma. Egypt was a good girl, but she was born in a fucked up situation. I hated seeing her being raised by that monster. That's why I was so hard on her, but she couldn't see that though. Like I said, I hated putting my hands on her, but that mouth of hers was too much sometimes.

"Didn't I say dry ya' fuckin eyes, huh?"

"Y-y-yes."

"Okay, so tell me why I still see tears on ya face then? Keep playing with me, Egypt. I swear you gon' make me beat ya ass like I'm your daddy."

"You already do."

"What?"

"It's bleeding! I said my nose is bleeding!" Egypt yelled, trying to hold her head back at the same time as she reached around into the back seat in search of Kiki's diaper bag.

*****

EGYPT

As soon as I grabbed the bag, I felt something scratch my hand from underneath the seat. I pulled it out to get a better view. My eyes almost popped out of my head as soon as I realized what it was. Dirty bastard. I knew his ass wasn't shit trying to accuse me of cheating, but he'd been the one out there doing his dirt the entire time. I couldn't believe his low down ass would even do me like this after everything we'd been through. It was okay though because this just made it much easier to leave his punk ass. I didn't need this shit anymore.

I opened the box and looked inside. Instead of rubbers, all I saw was a pair of purple and white lace panties stuffed inside. I knew damn well they weren't mine, and I knew Miss Dee's old ass wasn't hiding panties under her seat. I instantly dropped the box back onto the floor of the truck and put the diaper bag on my lap without saying another word for the rest of ride. I shot Peanut an evil look as I took the pack of wipes out and began cleaning my face up. About ten minutes later, we pulled up in front of my apartment building and parked on the side of the curb. I didn't even give him a chance to put the truck in park before I opened the car door and got out. I threw the diaper bag and my purse over my shoulder and slammed the door. That's just how mad I was. Every time you tried to be good to a nigga, they always went and did some dumb shit. Then he had the nerve to put his hands on me after he'd been out doing wrong. That nigga had issues.

"Yo! What's your damn problem, girl?"

I didn't answer. I just opened up the back door and unbuckled the car seat, then I took it out and sat it on the sidewalk next to me. I reached back into the truck and grabbed the condom box off of the floor and slammed the door so hard that the SUV rocked from side to side. I leaned over into the passenger side window and just stared at me for a minute.

"What? You got something to say? I'm getting sick and

tired of your crazy ass attitude."

I just stood there quietly, then I slowly picked up the car seat and turned back around to the window. I stared him down for a few more seconds and then out of nowhere, I threw the box in his face and walked away.

"What the fuck wrong with your crazy ass?" Peanut yelled, but I just kept a steady pace, hoping he didn't decide to chase after me.

"Shit, I ain't stopping until I reach the front door," I whispered to myself. I could still hear him cursing and yelling my name, but I just kept on walking. There was no way I was turning around. I was done with his ass for real. I didn't even care, and nothing was going to stop me from finally standing up for myself. As soon as I got to the big metal door, I put the key in the lock quickly. I turned around and glanced quickly one last time, just to make sure Peanut wasn't coming behind me. No one was behind me, so I hurriedly ran inside and locked the door. I put the car seat on the floor and slid down the door until I felt the soft carpet underneath my butt. I glanced over at Kiki to make sure she was okay, and then I finally exhaled when I heard the screeching from Peanut's tires as he took off out of the parking lot. I knew he was beyond pissed, but I didn't care. Hell, it wasn't like he gave a damn about how I felt.

CHAPTER 4

EGYPT

I was still sitting on the floor with my back against the door when I heard someone turning a key in the lock above my head. I looked over at the clock on the table and read the time. It was 7:25 p.m. I couldn't believe two hours had passed by with me just sitting on the floor thinking. My mind was in a million places. I was trying to figure out which little bitch Peanut's trifling ass had been creeping with, and for how long. That nigga thought that just because I was young that I didn't have common sense, but I had news for his ass. I would show his ass that I didn't need him. I jumped up off the floor and headed down the hall to my bedroom. I knew it had to be my mom coming in because Paris texted me that she was spending the night with her boyfriend, and to tell momma that she was studying. Kiki must have woken up when I picked up the car seat because she started grunting and stirring around. I was almost to my room door when I heard my momma opening up the front door.

"Shit."

"Oh hell no, I know damn well you ain't keeping that crying ass baby tonight. I'm not in the mood for all that fuss."

"Well, hello to you too, Mommy!"

"Ain't no damn hello; you heard what I said, you little bitch!

You might as well call that little slut right now and tell her to come get this little hollering ass baby. Now!"

"Dang Momma, she's only spending the night. You act like she's staying forever."

"You better watch your damn mouth, bitch, before I throw both y'all asses out on the damn curb. Keep trying to be smart. You must have forgotten who the hell you're talking to, little girl. If you smelling your stank ass, you better go wash it. You hear me, bitch?" yelled Nadine as she stood in the middle of my bedroom floor with her hands on her hip.

"Yes, ma'am!"

"Yes ma'am my ass. Sitting around here acting like my house is a damn daycare! You must have started paying some bills around here; hell, you always bringing in extra mouths to feed like you buy shit up in here. If it ain't that baby, it's her damn momma! I'm getting sick of this shit, and where Paris little hot ass at?"

"I don't know. I haven't talked to her since she texted me earlier and said she was gonna be studying with one of her classmates after school or something like that," I lied.

"Um huh, studying my ass. She think her little ass smart. She thinks I don't know that she's laying up with a grown ass man and shit. I tell you what, though; let either one of y'all stank asses fuck around and get pregnant. I damn sho' ain't taking care of it. I'm done raising babies. You can sit there and practice with that little baby right there all you want to, but I mean what I say."

"I'm gonna finish school and get me a good job, and then I'll find a good man that loves me so we can take care of our babies together. Plus, I'm not even thinking about having kids anytime soon. I'm only watching her because Ari got something very important to handle in the morning."

"Yeah whatever, you ain't gon' do shit. Your dumb ass is gonna end up being a little hoe with a house full of kids, and your stupid ass sister gon' be right there beside you. Neither one of y'all asses will be shit. You gon' be stuck right here with me forever!" Nadine yelled as she pulled a glass crack pipe from her jacket pocket and put it to her mouth. I saw a trail of smoke follow behind Nadine as she walked down the hallway laughing. I ran over and slammed my door shut because I didn't want Kiki breathing in the fumes. Nadine didn't care who she smoked that shit in front of.

CHAPTER 5

PARIS

The sun was beaming down bright as hell today as I drove down the crowded block on Woodcrest. The block was popping. Anybody who was anybody was on Sunset today. It was the hottest block in Patterson, especially in the summertime. Everybody usually hung out on the block during the day, and then hit up this little club out in Rochester called The Spot at night. I'm Paris Parker; Egypt and I are twins, as she told you earlier. We both shared the same green eyes. She's a little shorter than me by an inch, standing at 5'5. I was what you call thick; not too fat, but not too thin. I had long curly hair that I recently dyed bright red. I guess it was because I liked to be different. Egypt, on the other hand—well, she was slim and short with a nice shape as well. I guess you could say we were double the trouble. We got much love in the hood whenever we stepped out. I just wished my mom treated us like that. I remember she used to treat us very well at one point. She wouldn't let a soul mistreat us.

I was always told that I was the spoiled one growing up; Mommy's favorite little girl. I could tell that Mommy treated me differently from E; Egypt was always a daddy's girl. She followed him everywhere he went. Momma hated that. She couldn't stand the fact that their bond was so tight. I remember she even tried to accuse him of molesting us once, just so that he would stop spending so much time with her. The police came and took us to the hospital, but they couldn't find any physical evidence that he touched us, so the case was thrown out. My momma always had a crazy ass way of thinking, and it got even worse when she mixed whatever drugs she took with it.

My dad was a great father to the both of us. He didn't deserve to be taken away from us in such a harsh way. He did a lot of good for everyone he knew, and for a stupid drunk asshole to take his life was just unacceptable. He robbed us of our happy home. Egypt and I were nine years old when he was killed. Our lives changed drastically after that day. My mom lost our house a few years later because she blew all of my dad's insurance money on crack and partying with her so-called friends.

Egypt and I got $20,000 each put up in a trust fund for us that we couldn't touch until we turned 30. I guess that was my dad's way of making sure we got our money just in case anything ever happened to him. I knew for a fact we wouldn't get to see a dime of that damn money if he hadn't set it up that way. I think that's why Momma was so scared for us to leave. She knew we have that money coming to us. He was a smart man and even in death, he made sure we were straight. I knew he was turning over in his grave when he saw the way my momma has us living. I missed him so much.

I know you're not supposed to question God, but I just couldn't help but wonder why he had to take my daddy away before I even got a chance to fully know him. That pain would never end. I knew he didn't mean to leave us all alone with our crazy ass momma. I didn't blame him one bit. It wasn't his fault she lost the house he bought her. She owed back taxes from not keeping up with the bills. Daddy had done his part. He left enough money to make sure we were good for years. We stayed here and there after that. She moved us in and out of the slums. I had never even seen an apartment building until then. Things quickly turned from good to bad to worse for us.

I could even remember when we were a little younger, my momma used to leave us for days at a time without food, lights, or water in the house. Egypt had to step up and take care of us like an adult when she was only a kid herself. She had to grow up before her time. She made sure I never missed a day of school, even though she didn't go like she was supposed to. I never knew where she found the strength to keep everything together. If it hadn't been for Egypt, I don't know where we would be right now. We never had company over because momma would lock herself inside of her bedroom for days without even eating. We could hear her just kicking and screaming. I didn't understand why at first, but I soon realized those were the times she was coming down off her high.

My momma would do anything she could to get high. The worst thing I could remember her doing to us was letting grown ass men come into our room and molest us. Well, they never got a chance to touch me because Egypt wouldn't let them. She made me hide in the closet until it was over. I would sit in there for what seemed like forever, crying my heart out as I listened to my sister scream and call for Daddy to save us, but it just fell on deaf ears. I hated that I was too young and weak to help her, and that just made me hate my momma even more. I knew right then she had no love for us anymore. It was all about the drugs. We had lost the mom we once knew. The sound of "Flex" by Rich Homie Quan snapped me back to reality.

"Oh shit!" I said aloud as I looked down at my phone and saw I had missed a call from Egypt. I quickly touched her name on the screen to call back.

"Wassup, sis?"

"Hey, where you at, P? Momma in here going crazy because you're not home, plus I'm babysitting Kiki and that doesn't make it any better."

"Oh my God! Ugh, she always snapping about something. I'm over on Woodcrest. Aww, and kiss my baby for me," I said, making kissing sounds through the phone.

"What in the world are you doing way over there? I done told your ass about driving around without a damn license. You ain't gon' learn until they lock your ass up. You already know how these Jersey cops are. They'll take you to jail for anything."

"Whatever girl, hush all that fussing. I got this, I know how to drive."

"That's not the point! You still don't need to be driving around at 16 without any papers. You so damn hard headed, and I swear you never listen."

"I hear you, E; damn, I'm just going to meet up with Dominic. I haven't seen him all day, and I went by his crib to see him after school and he wasn't home. So I jumped in the car to go see if he was on the block."

"Um huh, well you better be careful because you know it's hot on the block too. Don't make me have to fuck somebody up! I'm already having a bad day, so it's nothing."

"Ha ha ha, calm your little gangsta ass down, girl. Everything is cool, sis."

"I'm serious. You better call me if you need me. I'm not playing either, P."

"I'm good but if I need you, you'll be the first one I hit you up."

"Aight, well what you want me to tell Momma?"

"Just make up something, E! I'll be in later, just keep your phone on."

"Okay, talk to you later, love ya!"

"Love you too," I managed to say before the call ended. I checked my notifications to see if Dominic had texted me but to my surprise, he still hadn't. I tossed the phone onto the seat and turned the radio back up. I was just cruising down the block with the speakers booming. I had no idea my whole world was about to change forever.

I was dating one of the sexiest, hood nigga in town. His name was Dominic Taylor. He was 5'9 with light skin and shoulder-length dreads that he recently started growing. That nigga kept a mouth full of gold, and you never saw him with the same pair of sneakers on twice. Every hood nigga wanted to be him, and every hood chick wanted to get a piece of his pie. They already knew he was a young nigga getting money, and they tried every chance that they could to get in his pockets. Even though I don't have much I never asked him for anything. I guess I didn't wanna come off as needy. That's a trait Egypt and I both share. I never even invited him to my house because I didn't want him to see how I lived. Deep down I think the reason I never told him my situation is because I was too ashamed. I was used to seeing chicks flocking all around him, whispering in his ear. It was nothing! I even walked in on this one broad trying to give him head. I whooped that bitch's ass! Unlike Egypt, I not nice and easygoing. I'd fight anybody! I didn't care who they were. You fucked with me, your ass could get it. Straight like that. He already knew that I was crazy as hell, and I didn't care who knew it. I bet he never disrespected me after that, at least not that I know of.

Now, no matter how many hoes came around, he only had eyes for me. I was his world as he was mine, or so I thought. All that changed on June 12, 2005. That's a day I would never forget. I could still remember it like it was yesterday. I spotted Dominic's black 2009 Mustang parked in front of Halsbury apartments. Most of the apartments in this building were used for trap houses by the little young hood niggas. Most of them were mainly trapping out of their baby momma's crib. That's how it was in the hood. Everyone was looking for a come up by any means necessary. For some reason, it didn't feel right seeing him there because I had never seen him do business with anybody in that building. I knew all his connects and trap spots, and this wasn't one of them.

Something isn't right about this, I thought as I pulled up behind his car and shut off the engine. I got out of the car and walked up to the driver side door, just to double check that this was Dominic's car. I had to make sure I wasn't tripping. Just as I thought, it was his damn car because I recognized the broken passenger side door handle that he broke during one of our arguments. All kind of shit started running through my mind. I started looking around trying to see if I saw him somewhere standing around. Nope! I didn't see him anywhere, so I decided to go inside the building and take a look around. I headed over toward the double glass doors and pushed them open. The smell of cigarettes and urine hit my nose hard soon as I stepped inside. I looked around and saw a couple of crack heads sitting on the stairs leading to the first floor. I recognized one by the name of CiCi. Her and Momma used to be friends. She was sitting on the top step with a long cigar hanging out her mouth.

"Yo CiCi, is that you?

"Yeah, why? Who wants to know?" she replied, walking down to where I was standing.

"Hey, what's going on? It's me, Paris. Come here, let me holla at you for a sec."

"Oh Paris, that's you? What you doing on my side of town? How ya momma doing?" She still call herself mad at me?" CiCi asked as she walked up to me.

"I'm just chilling. I stopped by to meet up with somebody. Momma is doing good. I'll tell her you said hey."

"Oh okay, that's good to hear. Make sure you tell Nadine I asked about her."

"Okay, I sure will."

"Aye, let me get a dollar, Paris!"

I swear CiCi ass was always begging. I knew it was coming. I just shook my head, reached into my pocket, pulled out three balled up ones, and handed them to her.

"Thanks, P! You're such a sweetheart."

"Oh, it's no problem. Aye, have you seen Dominic around? He told me to meet him here, but he's not answering his phone. I don't know what apartment he's in," I lied. I knew if he was around, CiCi would tell it. She couldn't hold water. That was one of the main reasons her and my momma fell out years ago.

"Oh, Dominic? Yeah, I saw him come through about an hour ago. I think he went up to the third floor."

"The third floor?"

"Yeah, my little Cousin Pete say they be hangin' out in 302 with some new dude from Texas or somewhere. He just moved in about a month ago. Word is, him and his two cousins stay there together. From what I heard, he's supposed to be some big time cat from down south. I don't know what they got going on up there."

It was funny that I had I never heard him mention any of them. Dominic told me everything. He never kept secrets from me.

"Okay, thanks! 302, right?"

"Yeah, that's it!"

"Okay, I'll see you around the way!" I yelled as I headed for the elevator. I looked back and watched as CiCi and the other two guys that were sitting on the stairs with her dash out of the double doors, probably in search of their next high.

The elevator doors quickly shut behind me as I stepped inside and pressed the number 3 for the 3rd floor. As soon I made it to the top, I turned the corner and 302 was directly in front of me. The smell of weed hung heavily in the hallway. I stared at the door for a second, trying to decide if this was the right thing to do or not. When I finally got my nerves together, I knocked on the door twice, but no one answered. I raised my hand to knock again, but the door swung open revealing this tall, sexy, chocolate dude with dreads that were neatly braided into three cornrows.

"Can I help you?" he said, flashing a sexy smile with a mouth full of gold teeth showing. I was at a loss for words for a few minutes because that nigga was fine as hell. I almost forgot what I wanted.

"Um-uh yes. I'm looking for Dominic. My home girl said I could find him here," I lied again. I don't usually go around just lying to people, but if I want something, I'd say anything to get it. Before he could answer, a tall, skinny brown-skinned girl walked up behind him and started twisting her finger through the nappy curly weave she had in her head.

"Who the hell are you?" asked the skinny girl with an attitude.

"I'm looking for someone."

"Someone like who?"

"Yo, chill out girl; the bitch looking for Dominic," the tall dude said, nodding his head toward the side. The girl looked backed at me and smiled.

"Oh, okay; yeah, he's here. Come on in," she said, guiding me into the apartment like we were the best of friends. Just a few minutes ago, the bitch was rolling her eyes and shit like she had a problem or something. I wasn't sure what to expect once I got all the way inside. I almost lost my breath as soon as we walked into the front room. That's when I spotted Dominic. He was sitting in a chair on the balcony with his head back while some fat light-skinned bitch sucked his dick. I couldn't believe my eyes. The sight of it made me sick to the stomach. My blood started boiling instantly, but I had to play it cool, though.

"Oh, don't mind them girl! I'll go get him for you. Everybody love those trees, huh? Hell, we keep running out," the skinny girl joked as she walked toward the balcony door. She must have thought I was there to buy weed, but little did she know, shit was about to get real up in this motherfucka.

I walked closely behind the girl as she continued to talk about how in love Dominic was with the bitch that was on her knees sucking his dick

. "It's okay girl, I'll go get him myself. I bet he's gon' be so surprised," I told the skinny girl as I slid the glass door open and she turned around and walked back into the other room. They were so into it that neither one of them moved at the sound of the door opening, or me walking up behind them. Dominic must have felt my presence because he opened his eyes just as I pulled the pink pearl handle handgun that he had given me out of my purse.

"I had a feeling I was going to need my bitch today," I said as I pointed it in between Dominic's eyes.

"Paris! Oh shit, what the hell! How did—"

"Yeah, asshole. How do you think I knew where you were? Huh? Next time you decide to let a bitch suck ya little ass dick, how about hide ya fucking car first!" I yelled, waving the gun from him to her as I spoke. Dominic pushed the girl away from him as he stood up and fastened his jeans. The girl just laid back on the floor and stared up at the gun in my hand, then she jumped up like she was about to do something.

"Oh hell no, Dominic; who the hell is this little bitch? And why is she up in my cousin's apartment waving a gun in your face?"

"No, the question is who the fuck are you? And why you got your old fat, nasty ass mouth on my nigga's dick! I guess you like the way I taste, bitch!" I got all up in her face as I spoke. She kept backing up until she was against the balcony rails.

"Fuck you, bitch! It's so sad that you're so young and dumb. You think you're so smart, but you don't know shit about life yet. You think this nigga give a fuck about you? If he did then why is he here with me, huh?" she burst out laughing in my face. It's like that shit did something to me because I just snapped in the blink of an eye.

"You don't know shit about me, bitch! So shut the fuck up before I stick more than a dick down your fuckin throat!" I yelled as I pressed the barrel of the gun into her forehead with every word I spoke.

"Trust me, Miss Thang; I know more about you than you think I do. Who you think your man laying up with while your little young ass is in school?" she said, smirking.

"What's that supposed to mean, huh? What the fuck do you possibly know about me, bitch? And you're one bad ass bitch to stand in my face and tell me you fucking my nigga. I guess your bitch ass forgot I got a pistol to ya head. I should blow your fucking brains out right now!"

"Come on, P. Chill with that shit! Give me the gun!" yelled Dominic. "Steph, you shut the fuck up too! You run your mouth too fuckin' much. Damn!"

"Fuck you too, nigga! I'm not about to bow down to this stupid ass, wet behind the ear little girl because you're scared. You can't save every fuckin' body. You need to leave this charity case where the fuck you found her like I been telling your ass. I don't have time for this shit, Dominic. You said you were gonna handle it, so handle it nigga!"

"I told you to watch your fucking mouth, Steph! Who the fuck you playing with?"

"Or what, nigga? What you gonna do? I'm not sca—"

Wham!

I slapped the hell out of her ass with the butt of the gun.

"What the fuck, P?"

"That bitch talk too much. I'm tired of hearing her fucking mouth. I should have knocked all her fucking teeth out."

"Yo, you need to calm the fuck down and give me that gun. You waving that shit around all wild like you don't have any sense."

"So, is this what you want, Dominic? This is what you cheat on me with? An old ass, sloppy, nasty trick that's probably just after your money, huh?" I yelled as I pointed the gun at the girl.

"I thought you loved me, Dominic! At least that's the lie you tell me every time I see you. You said you wanted us to have a family together," Steph cried.

"Shut the hell up! You want some more?" I yelled as I turned the butt of gun toward her head. She stopped talking instantly, so I flipped it around. My hand shook nervously as I pressed it up against her temple.

"No more talking now, huh? Yeah, I'll teach you not to mess with me again, bitch! You're nothing but trash bitch. You're the bottom of the barrel. How are you gonna suck my man off knowing he has a girl? Your trifling ass. See, it's hoes like you that make all woman look bad," I said, smacking her in the face with the gun again but this time, blood flew everywhere. Dominic started tussling with me, trying to get the gun away from my grip. Boom! All of a sudden, the gun just went off. I was in shock. I wasn't trying to hurt anyone. I only wanted Dominic to see how much he hurt me.

"What have you done?" I cried.

"What do you mean? I ain't do shit! The fuckin' gun just went off, P! I told your stupid ass to put that shit down in the first place! Now look what happened," said Dominic, rubbing his temples as he spoke.

"It was an accident. I didn't mean for it to go off. It's all your fault. If your lying, cheating ass wouldn't have been over here, none of this would have happened. I knew your ass was up to something."

Out of nowhere, all we heard was BOOM! BOOM! BOOM! Then, the sliding door came crashing down behind us. Glass flew all over the place. The tall, dark-skinned guy who answered the front door earlier now stood in the middle of the living room holding an AK-47 rifle, pointing it at us. I was scared shitless. I'd never been in this type of situation before, so I was freaking the hell out. Dominic walked in front of me and used his body as a shield to protect me from the gun, but he knew just as well as I that one bullet would rip both our bodies apart at the same damn time.

"Yo—what the fuck, Trap?" Dominic yelled.

"What the fuck is going on, my nigga? Why is my cousin laying on the fuckin floor leaking from her head? Somebody better start talking right fucking now!"

"Yo' Trap, man let me explain. Bruh, it was a mistake. The gun just went off, man."

"Oh aight; a mistake, huh? Aye bae, get your ass out here now!" Trap yelled, looking over his left shoulder as he spoke.

Dominic stood in front of me and pointed my gun at Trap. I reached in my back pocket and pulled my phone out since Dominic had him distracted. I shot Egypt a quick text telling her where I was, and that I was in trouble. There was no use in calling the cops because it was going take them forever to come in this neighborhood anyway. Hell, they wanted us to kill each other. It was just another dead body to them. As soon as I shoved the phone back in my pocket, I heard the sound of a gun cocking behind us.

"Drop that shit nigga, or I'll blow both y'all fuckin heads off right here," Dee said in a low smooth tone.

CHAPTER 6

EGYPT

"Damn, it's about time you got your ass in here! I been calling you for the longest."

"Aaaaaaaahhhhhh, oh shit! What the fuck is going on? What the hell happened to Steph?" cried the skinny girl he called Dee; she came barging in the front room where the rest of us were standing, holding a double barrel shotgun.

"Don't act stupid! I know damn well you heard all them fucking shots. You got your stupid ass up in the room hiding. You know I'm gonna beat that ass when this is all over."

"Yeah, I hid like you told me to do if I ever hear shooting. Shit, how I'm supposed to know what was going on? I heard you talking shit, so I knew you were straight," Dee replied.

"Next time I call your name, you better come faster, but fuck all of that! These motherfuckas killed my cousin! Man, how am I gonna explain this shit to my momma? Oh Lord, Aunt Lisa is gonna have a fit. I was only supposed to bring her out here to look after her and make sure she stayed out of trouble. Fuck!" he, said pacing back in forth with the gun in his hand.

"What the fuck! Look, just calm down, okay? Please don't do anything stupid. Come on, baby; we moved up here to get out of that lifestyle. Let's not go back," Dee pleaded.

"How the hell do you expect me to calm down? Huh? Answer that shit. Stop acting fuckin' stupid and go grab the bitch and tie her ass up in the kitchen. I'll handle Dominic's bitch ass myself."

"Baby, what are you gonna do? Please don't," she begged.

I have no idea what this nigga had in mind, but it must be some horrible shit, I thought as I listened to the girl plead for him not to go through with whatever he had planned. My heart started racing, and I could feel my legs getting weak. I felt like I was about to pass out.

"Ain't you my ride or die chick?"

"Hell yea."

"Didn't you promise to do whatever I want, whenever I want?"

"Yes baby, bu—"

"Ain't no damn but! Get your ass over there and do what the hell I told you to do. What's with all this back talk lately? Keep playin' with me and I'll punish your ass next! Is that what the fuck you want?" Trap yelled.

"No baby, I'm sorry."

"Yeah, I know—now do what the hell I said before I tie both y'all asses up."

Dee walked over to me with the gun pointed in my face. She just stood there and stared at me; then all of a sudden, she jerked my arm and pulled me into the kitchen. I didn't put up a fight because I didn't know what she would do with the gun. She slammed me down into the chair, sending a jolt of pain down my back. I looked up and saw that Trap shoved his gun into Dominic's back and pushed him into the kitchen as well.

"Ouch. Uggh, you don't have to be so rough," I said.

"Shut your stupid ass up, bitch! This shit is all your fault. You have no idea what you've gotten yourself into. You fucked with the wrong people this time. Dominic should have been honest with you in the beginning, and all this shit would have been avoided But nah, you want to get my people involved in y'alls bullshit!" Dee yelled.

"Get your fuckin' hands off of her!" Dominic yelled.

"Shut your bitch ass up, nigga! I'll show you how it feels to watch someone you love die. You gon' feel my pain nigga," Trap said, walking over to me from behind, grabbing my ponytail, and wrapping it around his hand.

"Please, it was just a mistake! I'm sorry. I didn't mean to do it," I pleaded.

"I know, you said that already; but see, the crazy thing about me is that I don't give a fuck about what you did and didn't mean to do. You want me to have mercy on you, but my cousin over there laying in a pool of her own blood? What am I supposed to tell her four-year-old son who has to grow up without his mommy, huh? Too late for apologies, sweet pea," Trap said, yanking my ponytail hard. This time, me and the chair fell back onto the floor.

"Yo, chill the fuck out!" Dominic yelled, hitting Trap in the face and making him stumble backward and lose grip of the gun. It fell hard, making a loud "boom" noise against the concrete floor. Dominic bent down and pulled his .38 from under his pant leg. Damn right, I knew my baby never left the house without his piece.

Dee dove on the floor, grabbed Trap's rifle, and tossed it to him, but she was too late. Dominic pulled the trigger and sent five bullets crashing through his chest. Trap slumped down onto the floor instantly as the bullets ripped through his body. Dee came running from the other room with two big bags on her back. I didn't even see her leave the kitchen. She stood in the doorway silent and holding a 9mm. She had it aimed at Dominic and before I could say anything, she took one shot, hitting him in the head. He pointed his gun at her and fired once before he fell face-first onto the floor. Dee took off running out of the front door just as Egypt pushed past her and ran into the kitchen.

"Paris, is that you? Oh my God! What the hell is going on? I heard shots on my way up the stairs," Egypt said.

"Thank God, Egypt! You finally made it! Look, she killed

him! That bitch shot him in the head right in front of me!" I cried as Egypt ran up and hugged me tightly. I was covered in blood from head to toe.

"I'm so sorry, P. Come on, we have to get out of here. I know someone has called the cops by now. You know Dominic loved you more than he loved himself. He died protecting you, and you know he wouldn't want you involved in any shit like this."

"No E, I can't leave him like that. I just can't," I cried. Egypt had to pry my hands away from Dominic's body. I didn't want to just leave him lying there all alone on the floor.

"Look, we don't have time for this shit right now, Paris. We are in big trouble if the cops find us here. Do you want to spend the rest of your life in prison for murder? I don't think so. Now let's go, P!" yelled Egypt.

I finally stood up and looked down at Dominic, who was lying on the floor with half of his face gone. My stomach knotted up at the sight of it all. It broke my heart to have to leave him there. I didn't say anything. I just started walking toward the front door and then all of a sudden, it was like something wouldn't let me move any further. I stopped mid-step and just stood there. I tried to move forward, but I couldn't. Egypt was looking at me crazily when I turned around and ran back into the kitchen. I started going through all of the cabinets, yanking them open two at a time.

"What are you looking for?"

"This right here," I answered, holding up a big Ziploc bag full of coke.

"What in the world? How did you know that was in there?"

"I'll explain later. Go look around and see if you can find a big empty bag. Wipe off anything you touch!" I yelled.

Egypt returned with the big black duffle bag that had she found in one of the bedrooms. I had the whole kitchen table lined with money, weed, and coke.

"What the hell are we gonna do with all this? Have you lost your mind?"

"Just help me stuff it in the bags please, and stop asking questions," I replied in a calm tone.

Once we filled up the duffle bag, I threw it across my shoulder and went over to Dominic to take his car keys out his back pocket. Egypt grabbed the big black trash bag, and we hauled ass out of there. I could hear sirens in the background as we dashed into the stairwell and ran down the steps. We didn't stop until we made it outside. I tossed Egypt the keys.

"Here, you take my car and I'll drive Dominic's. Meet me at the old Towne Inn. Don't stop or talk to nobody!" I yelled as she ran over to the car and jumped inside. She started the ignition and took off down the road. I got in the other car and followed behind her until we got to the stoplight. Three police cars came racing past at full speed. I'm assuming they got the call of gunfire in the area. I made a left turn when I noticed Paris putting on her signal to turn right. I figured she was going the back way or trying to throw the police off. Either way, I wasn't chancing it. I dodged through traffic on my way to the interstate, checking my mirrors every second to make sure I wasn't being followed.

CHAPTER 7

EGYPT

"Can I get a room, please? If you have one on the back side, that would be great," I said to the desk clerk, trying to sound more mature than I really was. I was only 16, but people always said I looked older.

"Can I see your ID, please?" the old white lady asked as she typed on the computer.

I handed her the ID I had stolen from my mom. She never even looked up as she entered the information in the small laptop. I handed her the money and she gave me the room key. As soon as I got outside, Paris started yelling and cursing.

"It wasn't me. Blame it on the slow ass secretary," I replied, walking up to the car.

"I can't stand her stuck up ass. She always on that computer and keep an attitude."

"Ha ha ha. Hell yeah! Must be looking at porn or something," I joked.

"Girl, you a hot mess. What room we in?"

"G67."

"Good; that's on the back side, right?"

"Yep, I'll meet you around there," I said as I got into the car. I put it in reverse and followed Paris around the parking lot until we found the room number. We closed the curtains as soon as we got inside and locked the door behind us. Paris immediately started emptying the bags of drugs and money onto the bed, then she reached inside her purse and pulled out a small black scale.

"What you about to do?"

"I know we got over $9 million in coke and weed, but I'm not sure. I'm about to see how much it comes to."

"How you know about all that anyway?" I asked as she opened the bags and started putting the weed on the table.

"Come on, E; you know damn well what Dominic did for a living. He taught me everything he knew about the drug game."

"Damn, you never told me you sold drugs for him."

"Cause I didn't. He just taught me how to weigh and bag it up. You know, just in case I ever decided to do it myself. Hell, you already know Momma ain't giving us shit, and I'm tired of begging."

"I know that shit's right. Well, we don't have to beg anymore sis, 'cause we fucking rich!" I said in excitement. Paris and I jumped up at the same time and danced around. We were having a good time until I noticed she had sat back down on the bed. I stopped dancing too and sat down beside her.

"What's wrong, sis?" I asked, even though I already knew she was thinking about Dominic. My heart ached for her. I wish I could take her pain away. I could hear her sobbing softly as she hung her head down. I lay my head on her shoulder and cried with her. Neither one of us said a word. We just sat in silence and cried.

I had totally lost track of time until I heard my cell phone go off. I looked at it and saw that Ari had sent me a text, probably checking on Kiki as usual. That girl got on my last nerves with her calling constantly like somebody was going to hurt that baby. I was pretty sure she was sound asleep at my neighbor Tee Tee's house. I babysat her two sons on the weekends, so she had no problem with saying yes when I called and asked her to watch Kiki for a few hours. I opened the text and read it aloud:

"I need you! It's very important. Please meet me at the bus station at 10:30 p.m. tonight. I'll explain everything when you get here. Xoxo."

"Who sent that?" Paris asked, looking up through teary eyes.

"Ari. It sounds like she's gotten herself into some shit too. Damn, can this day get any worse? What is it now?" I huffed.

"Ain't no telling with Ari's ass. Some chick probably beat her ass again. She's always messing with somebody else's man," Paris said as she wiped the tears from her eyes with the back of her hand.

"I don't know. I just don't feel like any more drama tonight," I snapped, picking the stacks of money up of the bed. I started to count them.

"I don't know what to say about Ari, but in the meantime, I'm about to go holla at a friend of mine to see how we can get rid of all this coke and shit. We need to get rid of it fast."

"Aight, I'll be here counting this money. We've got to ditch those cars too."

"I've already got that covered. I'll be back later with a rental," Paris said, grabbing the room key and the bag with the coke and weed inside.

CHAPTER 8

ARI

I couldn't believe how fucked up my life had become. I'm Ari Ford, and from the time I was born, stones had been thrown my way. I never had much growing up, but my granny made sure my two brothers and I were straight. We lived with my grandmother from the time I was eight years old. My brother Mickey was four, and my baby brother Jashon was only a year old at the time. We had to move there because our parents had gotten locked up, so it was either my grandma's house or foster care, and there was no way that granny would allow that. My parents were sentenced to 18 years behind bars for grand larceny. It'd only been nine years so far, and I missed them so much.

My brothers and I wrote to my parents every week. It made us feel more connected to them. We used to visit, but money started getting short and my grandma couldn't pay for the trip to visit. We didn't hate them for what they did. The boys were too young, but I understood what was going on. Once I got older, my dad explained that all they were trying to do was make a better life for me and my brothers. They never wanted us to struggle like they had to. They thought stealing cars and selling them to chop shops was the easy way out, but it just landed them behind bars. It also put us in the position that they were trying to avoid the whole time. By the time they come home, Kiki will be all grown up. I took her to visit my mom for Mother's Day and to see my dad for Christmas, but she put up a fuss both times so I decided to wait until she got a little older before I took her back. My mom understood, but my dad? Well, that's another story. He asked about her every time he called.

"When am I going to see my grandbaby again?"

My dad was a mess. He was the nicest thug I knew. Before he got locked up, I remembered him tucking me in at night. No matter what he had going on in the streets, he never missed a night with his kids.

Life with my grandma wasn't all that bad, other than the fact that she lived in the projects. Everything in her apartment was top of the line. My grandma could have moved out at any time that she wanted to with all the money my parents had left her. She just chose to stay in that small, two-bedroom, roach-infested apartment. I had no idea why, but I guess she was just set in her ways. I moved out of her house when I turned 16 to go live with my boyfriend at the time. I thought everything was going good between us until I caught him having sex with the next door neighbor. I might have been young, but I damn sure wasn't stupid. His trifling ass had the nerve to try and convince me that she made him do it. I left his dumb ass and moved back in with my grandma. I had turned 17 by that time, and she was still trying to make me sit up in the house like a little ass kid. Being the sexy, wild chick that I am, there was no way that I was about to be stuck up in the damn house. I usually hung out with my three best friends, Paris, Rodney and Egypt. That's the only reason I like being at my grandma's. My ex was so jealous, and he didn't like for me to hang out with them.

The four of us had been friends for as long as I could remember. I think the twins were 12 years old when they moved into my apartment complex. Rodney didn't live by us but he came over to visit the twins often. The three of them were already friends before we meet. We all became close because we connected in so many ways.

I couldn't ask for a better friend than them, I thought to myself as I laid my head back against the headrest. My stop wouldn't be coming up for another hour, so I turned on my phone and shot Egypt a quick text for the fifth time. I knew I got on her nerves and it wasn't that I didn't trust her; I just missed my little boo bear. Kiki was my world! I loved her more than I loved myself. Being a single mother wasn't what I signed up for, but from the moment I looked into my baby girl's eyes, I knew I'd protect her with my life. Nothing else mattered. Kiki's dad was shot in the head by his cousin over a video game. Word got back to me that his cousin got mad that he had lost a bet over a basketball game. That's some crazy shit, huh? Your own family member takes your life over something so stupid. Sometimes, family isn't any better than a stranger off the streets. Where was the loyalty?

I was three months pregnant when Kelo died. He never got the chance to see Kierra being born, or watch her take her first steps. He was so happy when we found out I was pregnant. Damn, I miss my bae! I would always love him, even in death. He was definitely taken too soon. I had pictures of him all over my apartment because I still wanted Kiki to know who he was. Anytime she saw a picture of him, she said *"Dada,"* and it just broke my heart that she would never get to meet her daddy.

"The next stop will be Chicago, Illinois. Please gather all your personal belongings and remain seated until the bus comes to a complete stop. When we arrive at the terminal, please don't forget your bags under the coach. Thank you for riding Alpine Express, enjoy the rest of your day," announced the heavyset bus driver through the loud speaker.

I put my pink leopard print overnight bag in my lap and stuffed the headphones inside. Egypt would kill me if she knew I came all the way to Chicago to meet a dude I barely even knew. I'd met him online, and his name was Bryce Hemingway. We had been chatting for about six months over the phone. We finally decided to meet in person after all of this time. I knew if I would have told her where I was headed, she would have never agreed to watch Kiki. Not to mention, I would have had to hear her mouth. I was the oldest, but she acted like she was everybody's momma.

2 ½ Hours Later...

I sat in the bus station for almost three hours waiting on ol' boy to show up. I called him back to back, but he never answered. I was tempted to board the next fuckin bus back to New Jersey when he finally sent me a text. He said that he had gotten tied up and his phone had died. He promised he would be there in a few minutes. I didn't know what kind of women he was used to dealing with, but this shit was just unacceptable. So much for making a good first impression.

"Damn, it's about time you showed up! I was about to say fuck it and go back home."

"Pipe down, sexy. Look, I'm sorry sweetheart, I got tied up doing a few things. I was trying to get to you as fast as I could."

Damn. His lips were so damn sexy, juicy, and cherry red. The way he licked them when he talked just turned me on. This nigga was too fine. Just my kind of man. Tall, light-skinned, and with a low cut. *The things that I want do to him*, I thought as I watched the words just roll off of his lips as he spoke. There was no way that I could be mad at him.

"Um-huh, I hear you. I still don't like to wait," I pouted, trying not to give in so fast.

"Bring your sexy ass here, girl! You're too pretty to be acting all mean," Bryce said as he put his arm around my waist and threw my bags over his shoulder. He ushered me out the front door.

"Wow, Chicago is so beautiful at night."

"You think so?" he replied as we walked down the sidewalk arm and arm. He was such a gentleman.

"Yes! Don't get me wrong, I'm from the city too, but it's different here. All I see is police and ambulances up and down the street day and night. Niggas killing each other right in front of you."

"Well, it's not that much of a difference here. Chi-town gets a little wild at times too. I guess it all depends on what side of town you're on. You'll love the view from my house, though," he said as he opened the passenger side door of his Black and Silver Maserati.

"Damn, I like this car! What is it? A Maserati coupe, right? Probably got a 4.2 V8 under the hood, huh?" *This nigga must got cake*, I thought to myself.

"Wow! How you know all that? Ain't every day you see a chick that knows about cars. Hummm, I'm impressed," he said, looking at me and smiling.

"Yeah, well when you have parents that love to steal cars, you kinda get used to seeing all different kinds. I remember my dad used to take me along with him sometimes to case cars out. He knew the exact model of a car with one glance. All he ever read was car magazines, and he would sit me down and teach me about every car."

"Damn, that's deep right there, shawty. Shit, I wish my old man would have taught me something. At least you had him in your life.

"Well, not so much; my mom and dad both got 18 years in prison. My grandmother raised me and my two brothers."

"Dang, sorry to hear that," he replied as he rubbed his hand over my knee while he drove.

"Yea, it's okay. You live and you learn, right. At least he taught me something," I joked, and we both laughed. We chatted the whole way to his house. I learned a lot of things about him in just a short amount of time. I thought I was dreaming when he pulled into the driveway of the huge ass house that looked like a castle.

"Oh my God! I know this is not your house. Damn, you must be a doctor or something?" I asked, getting a little too excited.

"Ha ha ha Well, something like that."

"When I get rich, I want a crib just like this," I said, admiring the house through the window of the Corvette. "You stay here by yourself?"

"Yes baby, it's all mine. Come on, let's go inside. I think you'll love it even more."

I got out the car and walked behind him as we approached the big wooden door. He put some kind of code in a small keypad, and the door just popped opened.

"Wow!"

It looked better than any house I had ever seen in my life. I'd never set foot inside something so beautiful. It was just simply amazing. There were no other words to explain it. The ceilings were so high, and the stairs looked like they wrapped around about six times before you reached the top. It was just breathtaking. I don't know what he did for a living, but it sure must have paid a lot.

"So, how in the world can you afford a place like this, if you don't mind me asking?"

"We can talk about that later! For now, let me give you a tour of the house," he said.

For some reason, he kept avoiding my question. Every time I asked him what he did for a living, he would change the subject.

Bryce was totally different from any other guy that I'd messed around with. He was more mature. He spoke with manners and knowledge. I didn't take him as a street nigga. *He's probably one of those blue collar internet freaks*, I thought as I followed closely behind him, taking in the beautiful scenery as we walked. The walls were all white and trimmed in gold. Every picture frame had gold trimming also. He pointed out each family member in the pictures as we passed by and told me a little about them. I loved that he was so open about his personal life. White carpet ran throughout the whole house. I had to stop and just stare once we reached his bedroom. A huge canopy bed stood in the middle of the floor, which was made of all glass. Yes, other than the black throw rug at the foot of the bed, this man's entire floor was mad of pure glass. The bedspread and curtains matched, which were both all black too. This was the only room in the house that wasn't white or gold.

"Come inside. Have a seat," Bryce said as he pointed to the chair. "So tell me, what you think about my home?"

"I love every room. Damn nigga, you living like a boss."

"Ha ha ha; why thank you, Miss Ari. I'm glad you like it. Hopefully, you'll be spending a lot more time here with me?"

My mind suddenly drifted off to Kiki and the fact that I hadn't been completely honest with him when he asked if I had kids. It didn't matter anyway. I'd tell him when the time came. We just met, and I didn't want him knowing about my child until I got to know him better.

"Hey, did you hear me?" Bryce asked, waving his hand in front of my face.

"Oh yeah, my bad. You will most definitely be seeing more of me."

"Muah! That's what I like to hear," he said as he pulled me up from the chair and kissed me on the lips, then guided me backward until I felt the cold bed rail against my thigh.

"Ummmm, your lips are so fuckin soft," Bryce moaned as he sucked on my bottom lip; he slowly stuck his thick wet tongue into my mouth and started moving as our tongues danced around in and out of each other's mouths.

"I love the way you kiss me. Ummmm, you taste so good, Bryce."

"I want to taste you. Can I taste you? Please sit it on my face," Bryce begged as he put his hand under my shirt and massaged my breasts.

"Ummmm! Yes! You can do whatever you like."

I pulled the tiny blue jean skirt I had on down while Bryce took off my tank top and dropped it onto the floor. He then turned me around and smacked me on the booty as I climbed onto the oversized bed and hoisted my big, round butt into the air. He laid down flat and slid in-between my thick, wet thighs. I let out a soft moan as soon as I felt Bryce's tongue move up and down in my wetness.

"Oh yeah! Right there," I cooed.

"Ummm-huh, you like that?"

"Yessss! It feel so—"

POW! POW!

Boom! Boom!

CHAPTER 9

ARI

Shots were going off everywhere. Bryce jumped up and pushed me to the side. He reached under his bed and pulled out two double barrel shotguns. He yelled for me to hide.

"Get in the closet now! Press 102 on the keypad. Stay inside until you know it's safe to come out," Bryce said as he kissed me and ran out of the room, pointing the shotguns and ready to kill whatever came across his path.

I ran inside the closet like Bryce told me to. I didn't notice the small white keypad in the corner at first. Once I realized what it was, I ran over and punched in the three-digit code Bryce had given me. Suddenly, the wall started moving and a door opened up. I quickly ran inside and locked the door behind me.

"Fuck! What have I gotten myself into now?" I kept repeating over and over as I paced the floor of the small room. I could still hear the gunshots ring out throughout the house.

Boom! Boom!

For what seemed like hours, every time I heard a gunshot, I jumped because I just knew my life would be gone at any moment. I kept pacing around until I missed and bumped into one of the tables that was lined up against the wall with computer screens on them. I didn't notice it at first because I was too shaken up. I moved the small mouse, and all of the monitors came to life at once. Smart idea; Bryce had the entire house surrounded with cameras. I guess this was his little safe room. I looked at each screen and saw the masked men dressed in all black running throughout the house shooting. They were everywhere.

"What the fuck is this nigga into?" I whispered as I zoomed in the camera that was labeled *front room* to get a better view. It looked like something out of a western movie. They all had their guns pointed. I screamed when I saw one of the men hit Bryce in the back of the head as he snuck up behind him. He never saw it coming. He stumbled forward, but caught his balance quickly and took off running as bullets flew past his head. He was dipping and dodging every bullet until all of a sudden, I saw Bryce's body hit the floor instantly. Two of the masked men walked up and stood over his body. They sent two more shots into his chest. I couldn't believe what had just happened. They just killed him in cold blood right there in the kitchen. I looked back at the front room camera and saw one of the masked men standing by the fireplace. He was trying to punch the code in the tiny keypad beside the mantelpiece. He tried and tried, but couldn't seem to get it right.

"This nigga got secret rooms all over the place," I said to myself.

The other four masked men that hadn't been killed walked into the front room where the guy was trying to put the code in. I couldn't hear what they were saying, but I knew it wasn't good. One of the men pulled the trigger and shot the man in the back of the head as he punched the numbers in the keypad for the last time. The other four masked men ran out of the house without even looking back. I didn't know what to do. I sat there and stared at the monitors, trying to make sense of what had just happened.

"Think! Think! What am I gonna do? I can't call the police. How am I gonna explain this?" I looked around the room like the answer was just going to pop out of the walls or something. I stood up from the chair and started popping all the VCR tapes out. I gathered all of them up, pushed the code into the keypad, and ran out of the room back into the empty closet. I pushed the closet door open, ran over, and grabbed my clothes off the floor. I was naked the whole time. After I got dressed, I quickly grabbed the tapes off the bed and ran downstairs.

The house was silent except for the beeping noise from Bryce's alarm system. I walked into the kitchen, where Bryce had just been shot. I kneeled down and put my hand on his neck to see if he was still alive. He had no pulse.

"Damn, as soon as I find somebody I like, something always happens," I whispered. I got back up off the floor and started looking around for a bag to put the tapes into. As I began to walk out of the house, a thought pooped into my head, so I turned around and walked to the front room. I stood there and stared at all the blood everywhere. I held my breath as I stood over the dead masked man lying in front of the fireplace with his head blown off. I slowly punched in the same three-digit code Bryce had given me earlier. The beeping noise stopped and the fireplace began to open up.

My eyes almost pooped out of head. I looked at all the stacks of 100s, 20s, and 50s. The room was the same height as the huge six-foot fireplace and was filled to the top with money.

"Damn, so that's what their asses were after," I whispered as I ran back into the kitchen and grabbed some more grocery bags out of the pantry. I filled up as many bags as I could carry. I took the clothes that I had packed in my suitcase and threw them into the garbage, then filled it with money too. Once I had all I could carry, I ran out of Bryce's back door full speed. I could hear dogs barking in the distance, but I just kept on going. I ran and I ran. I never stopped until I saw this little diner sitting off by itself on the back road that I was running down. I had no clue where I was, so I couldn't call a cab to come and pick me up. This was the first time that I saw a building since I had left out of the subdivision where Bryce lived. That was about two hours ago. I walked inside the diner and looked around before I took a seat in the back next to the jukebox. As soon as I sat down, the waitress came rushing over to my table.

"Hi, my name is Maxine and I'll be your waitress this evening.

How can I help you?" asked the young white girl as she stood in front of me with her pen and pad out to take my order.

"I'll just have a Pepsi. That'll be all. Thanks."

The waitress walked away with my order, so I got up and walked to the bathroom. I reached inside my purse and took out my cell phone. I scrolled through my contacts until I saw Paris' number. My hands were shaking so badly that I almost dropped the phone. I touched her name and waited for her to pick up. Paris answered on the second ring.

"Aye, what's up chick? You good?"

"Not really, but I'll explain later. I need a big favor from you."

"What's up?" Paris asked.

"You think you can get the car tonight? I need you to pick me up?"

"Yeah, I got the car now; why, what's good Ari? Where you at?"

"I'm not in town right now. I need you to be at the bus station at 3:30 a.m. Egypt is supposed to be meeting me up there, but I don't want her catching a cab that time of night.

"Three in the morning?"

"Yes, P; that's the earliest that I could get a ticket for. Come on, now; don't act like that. Haven't I always come through for you? This is very important, Paris. If it wasn't then I wouldn't have asked, and you know that."

"Damn, Ari. Yeah, you know I got you girl."

"Look Paris, I really appreciate it. I didn't know who else to call and you're the only other person that I could ask. It ain't like Egypt has a car. I know Dominic lets you drive his car, so that's why I called you."

"Well, I got a rental car at the moment, but I'll explain all of that when I see you, and that damn bus better be on time too. Ain't nobody trying to wait all night." Paris and I talked a few more minutes before I hung up. I just stood in front of the sink and looked at myself in the mirror. Egypt and Paris were never going to believe this shit.

"We're fuckin rich!" I yelled at my reflection in the mirror, and then burst out laughing.

Knock. Knock.

"Hi, is everything okay in here?" asked the same waitress that took my order. She peeped her head inside the bathroom door.

"Yes, I'm fine. Thanks, I was just on the phone. Sorry if I was being too loud."

"Okay, it's fine. I was just checking because I heard some

noises. I just wanted to make sure you're okay. That's all."

"Oh okay, thanks again," I said to the waitress as she closed the door. I walked out shortly after. When I got back to the table, I waved her over and asked if she could write the diner's address down for me. I used my phone to Google local Chicago cabs, hoping to find one close by. Once I found the number I was looking for, I dialed it and asked for a cab to pick me up at the location the waitress had written down. The cab showed up less than 10 minutes later. I paid for the drink and left.

CHAPTER 10

PARIS

I looked at the clock on the dashboard and saw that it was almost three o'clock in the morning. I pulled into the bus station, and Ari was getting her bags from under the bus. I parked the car and walked over to help her with the bags.

"Hey girl, what you doing with all these damn bags?"

"Hey, P! Whooh girl, I'm so glad to see you," Ari said as she hugged me tightly.

"Well hey, I'm glad to see you too. I just saw you Friday. You act like you haven't seen me in years," I said as I took one of the duffle bags out of her hand and walked toward the car.

"Dang, Dominic ass keep a new ride," Ari said as she opened the door of the 2016 Escalade and climbed inside.

I didn't know how to respond, so I just got in the driver's seat and started the SUV. I turned the radio up and bumped the new R. Kelly CD all the way to the motel.

"Why are we coming here? I need to go by my house real quick."

"Hold on, we got to pick up Kiki and Egypt first."

"Why, what are they doing here? Y'all momma must have

been trippin' again?"

"No, Ari. We'll explain it all when we get to your house," I said as I got out the truck and walked to the hotel door. About five minutes later, Egypt and I came walking out. I was carrying the car seat with Kiki strapped in, and Egypt was carrying the bags. As soon as Ari spotted us, she jumped out the truck, snatched the car seat from me, and ran over and hugged Egypt. I didn't know what had gotten into her lately. Before she left Friday, she wasn't doing all that hugging and shit.

Ari buckled the car seat in the back and got in on the other side while Egypt got in the front passenger seat. I put the truck in reverse and backed out of the parking space. No one really talked on the ride to Ari's house. I guess all the events that had happened earlier played in our heads as we all sat quietly listening to the music. Once we got to Ari's house, she just broke down. Before we could even close the front door, she started crying and telling us about how she met a guy from Chicago online, and had been secretly chatting with him for a few months. She also told us how she watched some masked men break into his house and kill him while she sat in a hidden room watching it all on camera. My mind was spinning because she just kept talking in circles.

"Damn, that's some crazy shit. I guess we've all been through some wild stuff today. At least you're okay," I said.

"Hell yeah, and what do mean? I'm pretty sure your day

doesn't even compare to mine. I went through hell today girl, and why were y'all in a hotel room? Why didn't y'all call me? You know damn well that y'all could have gone to my house. Grandma got my spare key."

"I know we could have, but we needed to lay low for a little bit."

"Lay low, why? What in the world happened?"

I rolled up a joint and started telling Ari about everything that went down earlier between me and Dominic.

"What the fuck? Are you serious? You're telling me that my nigga dead?" Ari asked through teary eyes. I couldn't help but break down too, and that made Egypt cry. I hugged her as we all cried together. I knew it hurt them too because they loved Dominic like a brother. He was family to us, and his death made each of us sad in our own way. We sat back, reminisced, and shed tears for Dominic. We smoked joint after joint, trying to get high enough to make our pain go away.

"Oh shit, I almost forgot the best part! Y'all ain't gon' believe this!" Ari yelled as she ran over, grabbed the pink duffle bag, and unzipped it.

"Look!" Ari said as she started tossing stack after stack of money on the floor.

"What the hell? Where did you get this from?" Egypt asked as she held a stack of hundreds in her hand.

"Well, I didn't tell y'all the whole story," Ari said as she explained the rest of the story to us. She made sure not to leave out a single detail. Egypt and I just stared at each other silently because we were in shock.

"What's wrong? Why are y'all just standing there looking like that?"

"Girl, you're never gonna believe this shit."

"What?" Ari asked with concern in her voice.

I didn't respond. I just walked over to where Egypt put the black bags and picked one up. I dug inside, pulled out a stack of 50s, and handed it to Ari. I saw how her eyes lit up.

"What in the world! Um huh, y'all are talking about me, but where did y'all get this shit from?" Egypt and I just looked at each other for a while quietly until I decided to speak up.

"Well, it's a little bit more to our story as well."

"Yeah, there sure is. Go ahead. I'm listening. So, what happened? And how much money y'all got?" Ari asked as she picked Kiki up and sat down on the bed to feed her. I started explaining everything that happened. I started from the time I saw Dominic's car parked outside of the apartment building and explained it all, up to how I found the cash and drugs hidden in the kitchen.

"Damn! This shit is crazy. How did we go from scraping up change just to get a dollar burger to having enough money to do whatever we ever dreamed of?"

"Exactly. So what are we gonna do?"

"I don't know about y'all, but I'm leaving New Jersey and never coming back," Egypt said.

"I'm with you on that," Ari replied as she laid Kiki across the small twin-sized bed that the two of them shared.

We sat around all day making plans on our next move. We knew the police would be hunting me down sooner or later for questioning about Dominic once his body was found. Not to mention, whoever the money and drugs belonged to would be looking for it soon too. We couldn't chance staying in New Jersey any longer, so we had to leave and never come back. The next morning, we packed all of our things up and hauled ass out of Camden, New Jersey.

CHAPTER 11

RODNEY

10 Years Later...

I sat in my $3 million house and stared out of the window at the beautiful view of the ocean. Sometimes, I just sat and thought about how far I'd come. My life was a lot different than it used to be. I wasn't heavy in the streets anymore. Don't get me wrong, I still made my money, but I just wasn't getting my hands dirty. I had little niggas for that now. I figured out a better way to make money instead of being in the streets hustling for nickels and dimes. My nigga and I came straight out of prison, opened our own tattoo shop here in Miami, and took over. We linked up with this cat named B from Chicago when we moved down here. He put us up on game and fronted us the bread to open up the shop. The only catch was that he wanted to use the shop as a front for all of the drugs coming and going out of town. It was dummy proof really. All Marcus and I had to do was run the tattoo shop and collect Mr. B's money when the drop off came in. Simple. Shit was sweet right now. I know I said I didn't like to get my hands dirty, but don't get it twisted. I was still that same nigga that would take a fuck nigga's dome off just for looking at me wrong. I was a beast with these hands too.

Let me introduce myself. My name is Rodney Jones. I'm originally from Camden, New Jersey. I was 17 years old when my dad and I left and moved to Richmond, Virginia. I had recently lost my mother and starting getting into trouble. My dad felt like I was acting out because of some of the friends that I hung out with, so he thought that if we moved then I would get back to the old Rodney. The old me was dead and gone, but Pops just didn't want to accept it.

After my mom's death, my dad instantly turned into a single parent. He was always in my life, but my mom took care of me, the house, and she worked. I felt so lost without my mom. She was the only one that truly understood me. My dad couldn't control me because he worked so much and was never home. I took advantage of that and began selling drugs and hanging out in the streets all day and night. The only time I came home on time was when my dad was off work. He was so routine, so I knew the exact time to be home. I didn't want him to know the kinds of things that I was doing. In his eyes, I was the perfect child. I could do no wrong, but nothing changed when we moved. If anything, it got worse. I didn't want him to see that side of me, so I separated the street life from home. Little did he know, I was the worst child walking the streets of Richmond. When I was growing up, I fought anybody. I let go of all of the anger that I had bottled up inside of me, from losing my mom to my dad making me move and leave my best friends, especially Egypt. That hurt just as bad as the day my mom died.

I thought about Egypt all the time. I was always wondering if she finally left New Jersey like she always talked about, or was she still trapped in her momma's house being used as a sex slave. I wished I could find her and bring her with me. I knew she would have loved that. I hated that I had to leave her. I hope she understood why I left and knew that I would never just forget about her like that. I went back to Jersey a few times to visit my aunt after we first moved. I tried to find her each time, but I came up empty. I figured they must have moved again. I missed her so much, and I wondered if she even remembered a nigga! Nah, I doubt it. She probably ended up married and forgot all about my ass. I often imagined how my life would have turned out if Egypt and I would have stayed in touch, and if I had never left Jersey or went to prison for ten years. I took it out on everyone that crossed me the wrong way.

Just the thought of Egypt made me smile. I never wanted to leave her behind, but I had no choice in the matter. My name was getting real hot in the streets, and my dad feared I'd end up dead or in jail. He was right, as usual. I knew it broke his heart the first time he had to bail me out of the county because he distanced himself from me. He claimed it was because I wouldn't stop selling dope, but I already knew it was because I wouldn't live the blue-collar life he always dreamed I would. Fuck all that! I was a thug ass nigga, and nobody could change that. When I did my bid, I had a lot of time on my hands to think. Life was crazy sometimes because if I never would have gone through any of that, I would have never met my right-hand man, Marcus. Let me tell y'all how this shit went down.

Marcus and I were cellmates in prison. We were both locked up on bullshit ass charges. I was 17 going on 18 at the time. I was the biggest drug dealer in Richmond and had the finest girl in town. She was this thick pretty ass Spanish chick named Marisol. She was 5'2 with green eyes and had the biggest butt I'd ever seen. No one could touch me. I had it all. Niggas stayed hatin' on me because I was a little young nigga with money, power, respect, and all the hoes I wanted. They bowed down at my feet. Those bitches did whatever I told them to do with no questions asked. Like always, all of that changed once I got locked up. That was the worst day of my fuckin' life. I was driving down Chestnut Street on my way to scoop up one of my little honeys that would put in work for me whenever I needed shit done. I would stop through from time to time to check on her and get a little head and then bounce. Shawty was too young to bust down. She was only 15, but she was so damn sexy. I told her she could only play with the magic stick for now. Damn, just the thought of how much she must have grown up by now made my mouth water.

So, I was riding down the street when I noticed Marisol talking to two Spanish dudes. I immediately became suspicious because I'd never seen those cats around there before. I pulled my car into the Checkers that was across the street and parked in the back where I knew I couldn't be seen. I sat and watched as the shorter dude put his right arm around Marisol's waist. She smiled and giggled as he pulled her closer and started kissing on her neck. I couldn't believe my eyes. This dirty bitch was playing me the whole time. Damn! I didn't even see it coming. She always acted like the quiet, good-girl type. She kind of put me in the mind of my home girl Egypt when I first met her. I think that was the reason I fucked with her in the first place. Now, Egypt was the wifey type. She would always be my dream girl.

My mind suddenly drifted back to reality as I watched the short, skinny dude kiss on my bitch. Not once did she try to stop his ass. I got out of my Mercedes-Benz and popped the trunk. I thought about getting my .38 out and blowing these niggas' brains out, and making her funky ass watch her little lover boy take his last breath. That thought quickly vanished once I turned around and saw the two security guards sitting in the drive thru waiting to get their food. I closed the trunk back down and started walking across the street. I'm not trying to catch a fucking pistol charge but I'm 'bout to teach theses motherfuckas why I'm nothing to play with. Ain't no bitch gone disrespect me.

"This nigga must not know who he's messing with; clearly, she hasn't told him who the fuck I am," I mumbled as I stepped onto the sidewalk. The nigga was so busy kissing and hugging that he never saw me walk up on his ass. The other slimmer Spanish dude wasn't even paying attention because he was looking down playing with the phone in his hand. I snatched Marisol by the arm, yanking her around to face me. I slapped her so hard that she fell on the concrete sidewalk. That was the first time I ever put my hands on a female, but she was nothing to me anymore. I hated the day I ever met her trifling ass.

"Yo, homes! What the hell, son!" the Spanish nigga that was kissing on Marisol yelled.

"That's what the fuck I want to know, nigga. What the hell are you doing with your arm around my girl?"

"Que' quiere decir, amigo?"

"I don't speak Spanish, nigga!" I yelled, hitting him with a two-piece in the face. The other Spanish dude rushed over and punched me in the jaw. The lick didn't even faze him. Marisol got up off the ground and started cursing and yelling in Spanish.

"Vete a la mierda, Rodney! Te odio!"

"English, bitch! I don't speak any damn Spanish. What the hell are you so mad about? You're the one out here like a little hoe kissing niggas and shit! Huh?"

"Te odio! I hate you! I hate you!"

"I hate you too, bitch! You was only a fuck! And it wasn't all that anyway, stanking ass hoe!"

As soon as the words left my mouth, I felt a jolt of pain run down my back. I turned around and saw the short dude holding a board with a nail sticking out of one side. All of a sudden, I blacked out and started beating the dude that was holding the board so bad that his friend ran off and left him. Not long after, a crowd of people started gathering around. People were holding their phones out and videotaping the entire thing. No one even tried to stop the fight until Marisol started yelling.

"Help! He's going to kill him!"

Out of nowhere, two female officers ran up and tackled me and the Spanish dude to the ground. They tried to break up the fight. The ambulance had to be called for the Spanish dude because I had beaten him so bad. He had knots and bruises all over his face. They hauled my ass off to jail for simple assault. I later found out that I had broken his arm and fractured three of his ribs. I was a minor at the time, so I had to go to a prison for youth offenders. I lost all my money and drugs because as soon as I got locked up, Marisol set my ass up and had all my trap houses raided. The police couldn't prove the drugs belonged to me, so they just closed the case against me. Still, the dirty bitch planted two kilos of coke in my room at my dad's house. I got charged with that because there was no way in hell I was going to let my daddy take the wrap. That bitch turned out to be a damn snake. I couldn't believe I actually thought I loved her grimy ass. It turned out that the Spanish dude I beat up was actually Marisol's baby father. Yeah, who would have known it, right?

She played my ass good. I had to give her that, and I didn't even know her ass had kids. I would have never guessed it, but sometimes you live and you learn. I was living proof of that. I learned the hard way that you can't trust a big butt and a pretty smile.

While I was locked up, I got jumped by a few niggas. That's how I met Marcus. When he saw those niggas on me, he came in and started whooping ass. That was one of the realest dudes I'd ever known. We were both two young wild niggas from the streets. We clicked the first time we met, which was kind of funny considering the situation.

CHAPTER 12

MARCUS

I'm Marcus Simpson, and I'm originally from Jamaica. My mother and I moved to Richmond, Virginia when I was 14 years old. It was just my mother and I until she met my step dad. He treated us good, and I loved him just like he was my real dad. He and my mother got married a year after they met and along came my two younger sisters. My mom was very proud of me for beating the odds and finishing school like she always dreamed. It was important to her because she never got the chance to finish school. The last time I saw my mom was the morning of my graduation. Before l left to go to school, I hugged and kissed her goodbye.

They were supposed to meet me at the high school later that day but never made it. My mom, stepdad, and my two six-year-old sisters were hit by a train while crossing the train tracks. I never got to see them again. That was the last hug I got from her. I wish I could have held her longer. I wish I could have tucked my little sisters in just one more time, or read them their favorite bedtime story. Their deaths scarred me for life. I used to dream about them every night, praying God would send them back to me. I missed my step father too. He loved me like I was his own from the moment he met me. He never mistreated or acted funny toward me. He was the only father I knew. My dad was never around from day one. He got my mom pregnant and ran off with another woman, leaving her to take care a baby alone at the age of 15. That nigga wasn't shit.

My mom and I basically grew up together. She was just a kid raising a kid all alone. In Jamaica, things were totally different because it was legal to marry and have kids at a young age. My mom worked her ass off by selling crops and doing laundry until she had saved enough money up for us to move to the States. My Uncle Carlos already lived in the States, so he helped us get passports and the legal documents that we needed. Once that was all done, my mom packed us up, and Richmond, Virginia had been my home ever since. Well, until I met my nigga Rodney. After my family was taken away from me, I had nothing else to live for. I said fuck college and started doing my thing out in the streets with my big cousin. We put work in for a couple of big time cats around town. That's how I ended up behind bars in the first place.

It all began when I was on my way to pick up a package from Atlanta. Everything was going well. I got down there safely, got the work, and was two hours away from the drop off when I noticed flashing lights in my rearview mirror. I was nervous as hell. I had never been in trouble with the police before, so I was shitting bricks. Not to mention, all the drugs in the trunk had my heart in my shoe. I didn't know what to do, so I did the only thing I could think of. I mashed the gas and tried to get my black ass out of dodge. I was losing them for a while until the damn back tire blew out on me and I lost control of the car. I hit a tree head-on.

Lucky for me, I had my seat belt on or else I would have been thrown through the windshield. I knew my mother had to be watching over me that day. Thank God the police were so focused on making sure that I was okay that they never even checked the car. The only reason he was pulling me over was because my tag light was out. Damn! All of that for a damn tag light.

Now, I was facing way more charges than a warning ticket. I was booked for driving with no license, failure to stop for a blue light, running three stop signs, and reckless driving. Once they booked me, I was able to make a phone call. I hit my partner up so he could go get the car out of pound for me and finish the drop-off. We made sure to talk in code, so I wasn't worried about the police hearing shit. Man, those pigs stuck it to my ass. They gave me ten years with two years of probation after my release. I was doing good, just minding my business staying out of trouble, until one day it all changed.

I was sitting in the dayroom watching TV when I heard cursing and yelling. I looked over to my right and saw two young niggas fighting with no guards in sight. I tried to ignore it, but one of the guys looked familiar to me. He looked like this cat that I used to cop weed from on the west side from time to time named Rodney. We never really kicked it, but he was cool with my little cousin. They did business together. I heard he was moving big weight. Hell, I knew if he was messing with my peoples like that then he was really making bread. I heard about him around town too, and that nigga could throw hands. I hadn't heard of anyone that fought him in the hood and won, but it looked like he needed my help on this one. That big nigga was handling his ass. I was going to let them fight a fair one until I saw another nigga jumping in to help his friend. I wasn't about to let that shit that go down, so I ran over to the small iron table that they used for the visitors' sign-in sheets.

I grabbed it and held it over my head as I ran up behind the biggest dude and slammed the table down hard across his back. His bitch ass yelled out in pain, but that didn't stop me. I raised it high over my head again and this time, I hit him in the head with it. He fell over on the floor crying like a little ass girl. I started laughing from the way he was squirming like a fish out of water. I picked the iron table up one more time, but this time I brought it down sideways, hitting the other dude in the face. Blood poured out all over Rodney as he scooted backward on the floor, trying to get out of the way of the swinging table. I repeatedly swung the table, each time connecting with the dude's head. I beat his ass unconscious. Rodney finally got up from under the guy's limp body and started kicking him wildly. We beat them niggas until every guard in the prison pulled us off of them.

After about twenty minutes of beating us, they finally got us under control and threw us in the hole. It was dark and wet down there. I hated it. It reminded me of the house my mom and I used to live in back in Jamaica. Our lights were always getting turned off because my mom couldn't pay the bills on time. I could hear mice running around all night. I was always afraid of dark after that. I was afraid that somehow, those dirty, nasty mice would nibble and crawl on me.

Three Days Later

It was dead quiet in the hole, except for the crying and sniffling sound in the distance coming from the cell next door. I hadn't eaten since they threw us down there. I was hungry as hell. All that they gave me was two slices of bread and a cup of water in the last three days. I got up off the floor to use the bathroom and stumbled into something hard lying on the floor. I kneeled down and felt around with my hand. I jumped back when I realized it was a body. The room was completely dark, so I hadn't noticed that they put another person in there with me. They must have brought him in while I was sleeping. About an hour later, I heard grunting sounds coming from the guy on the floor.

"Aye, you okay man?"

He didn't answer. He only grunted louder.

"Aye my man, you good? What's your name, bruh? Come on, talk to me."

"Rodney. Ugh, my name is Rodney. Ah shit, these assholes

beat the shit out of me. Fuck, I can't move my arm. I think it's broken, man."

"Yeah, I know; they beat my ass too. That's why I'm in here, so stop whining like a little ass girl, nigga."

"Whatever nigga, this shit hurts! So I guess you're the little nigga beating motherfuckas with metal tables and shit. Huh?"

"Haha! Real funny, nigga. Look like you needed my help. Them niggas was on your ass," I joked.

"Whatever. I had it under control, nigga."

"Under control my ass!"

"What's your name anyway? You looked familiar as hell when I glanced at you the other day," Rodney asked.

"Yeah, I know you from over on the west side. I done copped a little bit of green from you a few times. I think you cool with my little cousin.

"Yo' cousin who?"

"Carlos from Petersburg. His baby momma live on the west side in the projects, and I used to see you out there doing your thing."

"Oh yeah, I know Carlos crazy ass. That's my little partner. I think I remember you now. Are you from Richmond? You sound like you got an accent, though."

"Yeah well, I'm originally from Jamaica. I moved here to the States when I was 14 years old."

"Oh okay, I thought I was trippin'. Well, looks like we're gonna be here for a minute. I guess we might as well get to know each other, huh?"

"Ha ha. You right about that."

Rodney and I sat and talked for hours about all kinds of stuff. We found out that we had a lot in common. His mom died too. He told me all about his dad and how he played professional football back in the day. Once I got to talking to him, I found out that he wasn't so bad either. He came from a good home too, but life just took ahold of him. It's crazy how stuff can have such a major impact on you. We were a lot alike in so many ways. He told me all about his friends up in New Jersey, which was where he grew up. The more we talked, the more we vibed and just like that, me and that nigga have been tight ever since. Rodney got out a year before me for good behavior. When I was released, we linked back up to move to Miami and we've been together ever since, just like Cheech and Chong. That's my nigga; wherever he goes, I go.

We started our own tattoo business together called Brothers of Ink. My nigga Rodney is a beast with the tattoo gun. I'd seen that dude put a whole city on a nigga's back. It was detailed and all. No one has skills like my nigga. Our little spot was the talk of the town. All kinds of major rappers had graced our doors. We even set up a little lounge area in the back, and that's where it all went down. You could come get a tattoo, hang out, listen to good music, and get blazed all in one spot. We were trying to expand and open up more shops around town, but we wanted to get this one booming first. We were close; it was coming, thanks to our new little business partner, B. That nigga had major dough. He was cool as shit too. I didn't trust his ass at first, but Rodney said he was good people so I trusted his word. He hadn't given me a reason to doubt him yet.

I swear life couldn't be any sweeter right now. I was making money the legal way, which helped keep my dirty money clean. Yeah, I know what y'all thinking, *"I knew he wasn't gon' change."* Well, you already know a nigga can't give up the streets that easy. It's in my bloodline. My momma hustled every day to make ends meet, so when I was left all alone, I had to do the same thing. I had to do whatever it took to make sure I kept a roof over my head and food in my stomach. I never depended on anybody for anything. I did whatever it took to get it. Rob, kill, or steal—it didn't matter. If you had it and I wanted it, you had better believe that I was coming for it. I was so glad that I didn't have to do any of that anymore because I was making so much money from tattoo business and the little side hustle with B that I would never be hungry again. I had everything a nigga could ever want. Now, all I needed to do was find a sexy ass chick with a big butt so I could settle down and make a few babies before it was too late. I wasn't trying to be in the drug game forever.

CHAPTER 13

ARI

"Kierra Arianna Ford! If I call your black ass one more time, I swear you'll be walking to school."

"I'm up! I'm up! Dang, Mommy! You ain't got to do all that yelling. Why are you taking me to school anyway? I thought Aunt Egypt was taking me today."

"Yeah, well things change. I'm off today, so I'm taking you. So stop asking questions and get dressed now, Kiki! That's your problem now, Egypt got your ass too spoiled. You're supposed to be riding the bus anyway."

"Ugggh, okay. I'll be downstairs in a minute, Momma," Kiki said, stretching as she stood up.

"You got 10 minutes, and I'm not playing with you either!"

"Okay. Okay, already. You see me getting my clothes. Dang, chill out Momma."

"Chill out? Have you lost your damn mind? Don't get your teeth knocked down your throat, little girl. Who the hell do you think you're playing with? I'm your momma, not one of your little pissy tail friends. You better watch your mouth!" I yelled, walking out of her room.

This girl thought she was a grown ass woman talking to me

like she didn't have any sense. She was going to mess right around and let her little friends get that ass beat for trying to do what they did. Kiki knew damn well that I didn't play with her. I tried not to be so hard on her, but look how out of control her mouth had gotten. She thought just because she'd be turning 12 next month that I wouldn't put my foot in her ass, but news flash sweetheart: this was my house. I paid the cost to be the boss in this bitch. She was going to abide by my rules until she turned 18, then she could do what she wanted. Fifteen minutes later, Kiki came running downstairs with her backpack, dressed and ready to go.

"You ready, Momma?"

"You ain't wearing that shirt, so you might as well go change it!"

"Ugggh! Come on, Mommy. There's nothing wrong with my shirt."

"I can see straight through it, so either put on an undershirt or take it off! The choice is yours. You got two minutes," I said as I grabbed my car keys off the kitchen table.

"Leave that girl alone, Ari. Why you in here messing with my baby?" Egypt said as she hugged Kiki.

"Hey, Aunt E! Good morning!" Kiki said, hugging her back tight and smiling from ear to ear.

"Good morning, sweetheart! You look very nice today."

"Thank you, Auntie. At least somebody likes it," Kiki replied, rolling her eyes as she walked out the front door and got into the car.

"See, there you go again, undermining my parenting in front of her! That's why she doesn't respect me now!"

"No I don't, Ari! You're just too hard on her."

"No I'm not! You just let her get away with whatever. If you let me raise her the way I want to, she would listen more. I'm on the way out so I'll call you later. I got to go!" I yelled over my shoulder as I walked out the door.

"Well, damn! What's your problem? Why are you so grouchy this morning?" asked Egypt as she followed behind me outside.

"It's nothing! I'll call you later!" I yelled as I got into her all-white 2016 Chrysler 300 and started the engine, leaving Egypt standing alone on the front steps.

*****

EGYPT

"Hey girl, what are you doing?"

"Nothing, just laying back, relaxing, enjoying my day off,"

answered Paris, sitting up on the couch so that I could sit down.

"I know that's right, girl. You so lucky; ugh I got to go in at 10:30."

"So why you up so early?"

"Oh, I just left Ari's. I was supposed to be dropping Kiki off at school but when I got over there, she was in one of her little moods. She was snapping at Kiki for no reason."

"Wow! You know how Ari can be sometimes. She must be done broke it off with Mr. Lover boy again. You know they were supposed to go to that R. Kelly concert last night, but he never showed up." Paris said.

"Oh yeah, that's right. I forgot all about that."

"Umm huh. She called me last night, crying bout' how he ain't shit and all that. I knew she was gonna be in a fucked up mood today. You know how she is when she get mad at that nigga," Paris said, pointing the remote at the TV as she flipped through the channels.

"Yep, take it out on us as usual."

"Exactly! Paris said.

"You'd think she would be happier due to the fact that she just opened her seventh restaurant in the Miami area."

"Say what?" Paris asked, surprised.

"Yep, I got an email today from our lawyer, and he said that her seventh one was approved yesterday. I was gonna break the news to her this morning, but she acting all stupid and shit." I said, kicking my slippers off.

"Damn, that's good! She's gonna be happy as hell when she finds that out."

"I know she is, but what are you doing on Friday? I was thinking about going out to celebrate and we can break the news to her then." I asked.

"Yeah, that's a good idea. It's been a while since we all went out together and just hung out. What did you have in mind?"

"Well, I was thinking about this new tattoo shop on Brookshire that I heard about from one of the girls that came by the salon. It's supposed to have a club in the back and she say it's packed with niggas."

"Say what? A club slash tattoo shop! That sounds ghetto as hell." Paris said, as she burst out laughing.

"Not really. I think it's a smart idea. Think about it: even if you're not getting tats done, you can still lounge in the back and have a few drinks. Plus, after all that pain, I'm pretty sure people want to drink when it's over. Smart. They making money both ways. Hell, I should have thought of that before I opened my other salon up. I could have invested in that." I said.

"Ha, ha, ha. Girl, you so silly. So what's the name of it?" asked Paris.

"I think she said it's called Brothers of Ink or Brothers Ink. I don't know, something like that."

"Oh, aight. Well, it might be cool. We can go check it out if you want to. I might go ahead and get tatted up while I'm there." Paris said.

"Oh Lord! Now, I don't know about all that. All I'm tryin' to do is get twisted and hopefully find a fine ass nigga to flirt with for the night. You know, nothing major," I joked.

"I think I might get it done, but I don't know yet. I'll let you know before Friday."

"Um huh, I hear you. Well, I'm about to get my ass to work before I lose all my customers. You know I need all the money I can get," I joked, as I grabbed my bag, slipped on my slides and headed for the door.

"Okay; see you later, sis. Love you!" Paris yelled, right before the door slammed.

CHAPTER 14

EGYPT

"Damn, Ari. All of your ass is hanging out of those shorts. This ain't no strip club."

"Shut up, Egypt! They ain't even that short," Ari said, pulling her shorts down on both sides as she walked.

"Um huh. I can see your whole ass cheek, girl."

"Well, why are you looking at it?"

"Hell, how can miss it? You're the one walking all in front of everybody, like I want to see your stank ass."

"Hush, E!" Ari replied, playfully punching me on the arm.

"Chill out y'all, dang! Y'all asses fuss like husband and wife," Paris whispered as she opened the door of the Tattoo shop.

No one was at the front desk, so we decided to take a look around. The tattoo shop was decorated with graffiti all over the walls. The carpet was bright red with black curtains, and the initials R.M. hung in-between each area. Some areas were sectioned off, making them private. Low, soft music played from the speakers on the wall. The atmosphere was so relaxing and calm. You would never know there was a club in the back if you didn't know beforehand.

"Hi, can help you?"

Paris, Ari, and I all jumped at the same time from the sound of a woman's voice coming from behind us.

"Hello. Um, yes, we heard about you guys through a friend and we wanted to come get a few drinks and chill. I was also thinking about getting some work done," Paris said.

"Oh okay, that's great! Yes, we have a lounge area in the back. You are welcome to go check it out. The food is really good too," the receptionist said, pointing to the doors at the far end of the building.

"Oooh yea, that's what I need right now!" I said.

"We also have a drink special if you're getting a tattoo done; for after you're finished, of course."

"Oh, okay. Can I take a look at some pictures or magazines?" Paris asked, "I don't really know what I want yet."

"Sure, follow me right this way," the girl answered.

"Aye P, we'll be in the back. I need a drink too, girl; it's been a long week!" Ari yelled as she followed behind me through the double wooden doors leading to the club.

"Damn, so that's how y'all heifers gon' be? Aight cool, I see how it is!" Paris yelled.

"It's nice up in here, girl. Look how big the dance floor is! I know they're making some major bread up in here. See, this is what I should have invested my money in," Ari said.

When we left New Jersey ten years ago, we had no idea where we were headed, or where we would end up. We just packed our stuff and left town. We never even went back to visit, not once. I knew our families were missing us like crazy, wondering if we're dead or alive. Well, my mom probably never even reported me and Paris missing. I knew Ari's grandmother was worried sick about her and Kiki. I hated that she couldn't at least say goodbye to her and her two brothers before we left. I knew they were heartbroken. We stayed in different hotels in different cities every night until we reached Miami Florida.

Oh my God, it was so beautiful! I loved it from the moment we arrived. I begged Paris and Ari to stay. They both agreed, and it had been our home ever since. Paris and I were still under age at the time, so Ari had to be our guardian because she was 18. Ari bought each of us our own house on the same block. When Paris and I turned 21, she signed the deeds to our houses over to us. We each started our own businesses. Ari opened up a small soul food restaurant, which had now expanded all over the Miami area. Paris started her own web designing company, and I'm in the process of opening my third salon in Atlanta. We had split all of the money equally and put it into three separate accounts. The three us even put $20,000 each into a different bank account for Kiki after she finished college.

"Yeah girl, this would have been a good idea. Shit, we could have even made it a strip club," I joked.

"Hell yeah! All male!" replied Ari, taking a sip of her Grey Goose and pineapple juice.

"Damn right! I wouldn't have it no other way."

"Oh yeah, I almost forgot to tell you the good news."

"What?"

"I was trying to wait on Paris, but oh well. Guess who got signed to another deal?"

"Who?" Ari asked with a confused look on her face.

"You. They approved you for the spot in Pamlico."

"Yes! Oh my goodness! I can't believe it. I did it. I did it!" Ari screamed.

Everyone in the club started staring at us like we were crazy. Ari yelled out for the bartender to bring us another round. We drunk two bottles of Grey Goose by ourselves. We were really turned up! I missed us having fun like this. It'd been a while.

I placed the empty bottle on the table and looked around the club. I noticed this one guy that kept staring at us. I've never seen him before. *Hmm, I wonder what that was all about*, I mumbled to myself.

"Girl, what's wrong with you?" Ari asked

"You see that guy over there in the corner?" I whispered, like he could hear me.

"Yea, so what?" she said looking over at him.

"I don't know. He keeps on watching us."

"Shit, I can't really tell how he looks from over here but it's been a minute since I had some so he better not be staring too hard." Ari said, as she turned the glass up and finished the drink.

"Um huh. Yo drunk ass already got a man. Come on, let's pay for these drinks and go check on P. It's been a couple of hours and she still hasn't gotten done yet."

"Okay, E. Hold on, let me get one more shot of goose," Ari slurred, as she waved the waitress over to us.

"Come on girl, you gon' be tore up drinking all that damn liquor."

Ari got up from the table and stumbled back down to the chair. I got up out my seat and walked around the table so I could help Ari stand up. She held on to my arm as we walked to the bar. I gave the bartender my Visa card and the bill.

"Thank you! Have a good night," he said as he handed me the

card back. I took it from him and stuffed it back inside my purse. Ari and I walked arm and arm out of the lounge area. I knew the liquor was starting to kick in because I could feel my head begin to spin with every step I took.

CHAPTER 15

PARIS

"Wow, that's beautiful!"

"You like it?"

"Yeah, girl. He's hooking you up."

"He needs to hurry up. I'm hungry, shit!"

"Hush Ari, ain't nobody tell you to drink all that damn liquor!

"I'm ready to eat too," Egypt said.

"I'll be done in about 20 minutes. Can y'all hold on that long?" asked the sexy brown-skinned dude doing the tattoo.

"I guess so. It ain't like we got much of choice, right?" Ari slurred.

"Sit y'all drunk asses down somewhere and quit rushing the man. Damn! Let him do his job!" I snapped.

"Thanks, little momma!"

"Aww, shut your black ass up! You just glad she keeping us off your ass!" Ari yelled as she tried to stand up, but fell back down in the chair.

"Nah, sexy. It ain't like that. I'm just doing my job. Y'all have no reason to get on my ass. It seems to me you had a little too much to drink, shawty," the tattoo artist said as he wiped ink off my shoulder blade.

"Don't pay her any attention. She's clearly had too much to drink tonight; actually, they both have. Good thing I'm the designated driver, huh?"

"Don't sweat it, ma; I understand. We've all been there before."

"Aye Marcus, you got 30 minutes 'til closing. Wrap it up, son."

"Aite. I got you, Bruh. I'm just putting the finishing touches on it. Yo, check out my skills. I told you ya boy can't be touched."

He leaned over and looked at the tattoo on my shoulder. It was two hearts with the words **PARIS AND EGPYT: A BOND UNBREAKABLE** in the middle.

"Paris and Egypt. Paris and Egypt," he repeated.

I turned around on the table to get a good look at the other dude because his voice sounded familiar. I jumped up off the table and hugged him. He just stood there for a few seconds, like he was trying to figure out who I was.

"Oh my God! Is it really you, Rodney? I can't believe it's really you!" I screamed.

"Paris? Damn, it's been a long time. What are you doing all

the way down here? How have you been, sis? How's the family?" Rodney asked as he hugged me.

"I live here now."

"Damn for real? With who? How's Egypt doing?"

"Her drunk ass over there," I said, pointing over to the where Egypt and Ari were sitting in the chairs passed out drunk.

Rodney walked over and tapped Egypt on the arm. She was so drunk she didn't even budge.

"E! Yo, E get up!" I yelled.

Egypt mumbled something and turned around in the chair, trying to get comfortable.

"Girl, get your ass up! It's time to go!" I yelled, yanking Egypt and Ari's arm at the same time. Rodney was standing beside me and as soon as Egypt opened her eyes, she started rubbing them. I guess she thought she was still dreaming or something.

"So I don't get a hello or anything after all of this time?" asked Rodney, not taking his eyes off of her as he spoke.

Egypt was in shock at first, then she jumped out of the chair and squeezed Rodney tight, a little too tight because Egypt vomited right there on the floor.

"Oh my God! I'm so sorry!" Ugh!" said Egypt, holding her

hand up to her mouth.

"Eeeew! That's from all that damn liquor you've been drinking," I gagged.

"Damn E, I see nothing's changed, huh? You still can't hold your liquor," Rodney joked, making everyone laugh.

"Shut up, Rodney. I see ain't shit changed with you either. You're still the same asshole you've always been," Egypt said as she staggered out off to the front door.

"Yo, chill E! You know a nigga was only joking with your sensitive ass!" Rodney yelled after her as she slammed the door shut.

"Don't worry about her. She'll be okay. Can you please help me take my home girl to the car with her drunk ass? I don't know why they drank so much. Knowing damn well neither one of their asses can handle it."

"Yo, ain't that Ari? Damn, it's been a long time sis. Come on, I was just leaving anyway. Yo Marcus—you gon' lock up, right?" Rodney said, looking at Ari passed out in the chair.

"Yea, I got it." Marcus yelled.

"Aight, I'm out. I'll hit you up later, bruh."

Rodney lifted Ari out of the chair and put his arm around her waist so that she wouldn't fall. He followed behind me out the front door. Once we got to my car, I held the door open while he put her inside and fastened the seat belt.

"Well aren't you such a gentleman."

"Don't start, Egypt. I'm only making sure y'all are safe."

"Um huh. I bet you are," Egypt said sarcastically.

"Here, take my number and stop being so mean. Hit me up and let me know y'all made it safely, okay?" Rodney said, handing Egypt a business card. Egypt snatched the card out his hand, looked at it, and then stuck it in her purse.

"Um huh. I gotcha." She said, rolling her eyes.

"Well, we're gonna get out of here, bruh. I'll make sure that she calls to let you know that we made it home. Oh, and tell ya home boy I love the tattoo. He did his thing."

"That's what's up, P. I'll be sure to tell him. Drive safe."

"Okay, Bye." I said as I looked in the rearview mirror at Rodney standing on the sidewalk.

CHAPTER 16

EGYPT

"Oh my goodness, girl; it was so good seeing Rodney last night. I swear he still looks the same."

"Yes, it was. I'm so embarrassed, y'all. I can't believe I threw up all over the place. Then he had the nerve to laugh. Ugh, he got on my nerves."

"No! I know you didn't?" asked Ari.

"Hahaha. Yes girl, that shit was crazy as hell. I couldn't stop laughing either. Rodney is a mess."

"Shut up P, it's not that funny!"

"Yes it is; and, Ari you can't talk because he had to carry you to the car."

"What? Damn, I'm never drinking like that again. My head is pounding, ugh!"

"Me either; my stomach and my head are hurting. I need some breakfast," I said, rubbing my stomach.

"You're going to make it? I'm surely not."

"Whatever girl, I'm not cooking anything. I'm about to take my ass to Waffle House."

"I'm going too," Ari said, grabbing her shoes.

"Here, get your phone. It's been vibrating all morning," Paris said, tossing the phone to me.

"Aight. We'll be back later," I said as Ari and walked out the door.

*****

RODNEY

"Yo, what's good Bruh?"

"Shit, trying to finish this last tat so I can get up out of here early tonight."

"Aw hell, you must got something planned with ol' girl?" I asked.

Marcus was dating this little stuck-up bitch named Monique. I couldn't stand her money hungry ass. She was always begging a nigga for a handout. Real niggas want real bitches; you know, the kind that can bring something to the table. Hell, I could get that whenever for free. I didn't like her because she was just trying to play my nigga and make him take care of her lazy ass. I had no respect for hoes like her.

"Yeah, she wants to go hit that little club up on the strip," Marcus answered.

"Man, you need to leave that hoe alone. All that she is doing is using you. You're just too stupid to see it."

"Whatever, nigga. Shut your hatin' ass up. At least I've got a girl, unlike you. So holla at me when you get one."

"Yeah, well fuck a bitch right now. I'm on some other shit, bruh. I don't have time to be giving away my paper to no hoe."

"Fuck you, Rodney! You're just mad. I've got who I want."

"Shit, don't worry about me. I'm good, my nigga. I get pussy when I want it. I don't have to house the hoes. That's your job."

"Fuck you, man! What do you want anyway? I'm busy."

"Mr. B sent me to holla at you."

"Oh yeah, come in the back real quick," Marcus said, walking off to the supply room with me on his heels.

"So what's good? Holla at me," Marcus said as he closed the door.

"I just got word that one of our trap houses in Jersey got burned down last night."

"Say word?"

"Hell yeah. B wants one of us to go up there and check it out."

"Shit, why can't one of them little niggas go?"

"He wanted to send a message, and he wants it to be loud and clear. Them little niggas don't know shit about putting in any real work. He wants the job done right."

"So what are you gonna do?"

"I was thinking me and you ride up there. We can lay low for a few days and scope shit out. Then, when the time is right, we'll lay them motherfuckas down one by one. We'll show them pussy niggas that we ain't anything to play with. I already hollered at some of my little goons from back in the day that used to put in work with me and they're ready for war, my nigga."

"Damn right!"

"Yep. I want New Jersey to beg for mercy. I'm tired of niggas thinking I'm a pussy. I took a major loss when I was in the pen. It took me a long time to put my trust in a motherfucka again. Things are gonna be different this time."

"I hear you, bruh. So when do you plan on taking that trip? You know I'm down for the cause."

"I'm thinking about leaving Monday night so we can be back by Thursday. I got a little something planned for the weekend."

"Oh yeah, like what?"

"I'm planning on having a little barbecue at my spot and inviting my home girls over when I get back in town. We've got to catch up. It was so good seeing them again."

"Yea right, good seeing them? Or good seeing Egypt?"

I couldn't sugar coat anything with Marcus. He already knew how I felt about Egypt.

"Both, actually. Paris and Egypt are my best friends. I've seen those girls go through a lot of shit, so to see them happy and still alive is all that matters to me. I told you how I felt about having to leave them back in the day. I wished I could have done more to help them."

"I'm sure they understand, and it looked like they're doing pretty well for themselves. So I wouldn't beat myself up about it if I were you."

"I don't know, bruh. I been trying to hit Egypt's ass up all morning, but she ain't even respond to a nigga. I know she's still mad at me for leaving without even saying goodbye. To top it off, I moved the day after we had sex for the first time. I know she looked at me like any other nigga after that. Damn, I never wanted her to feel like I just wanted to hit and bounce. She has always been special to me."

"Yea, she did seem upset with you when she left the shop the other night, and now I know why. Damn bruh, you might have messed up with her."

"Yeah I know, that's why I got to figure out a way to make it up to her. She just upset right now. She's just got to let me make it right this time. I haven't been able to get her off my mind since I saw her."

"Damn, she must be the one because I never heard you talk about a female like this before. She is beautiful, though. I can't even front."

"Damn right she's beautiful," I said, looking at my phone to see who had just texted me.

"Aye, I'll holla at you later, my nigga. I got to handle something right quick," I said as we both walked out the storage room.

CHAPTER 17

EGYPT

I'd had a lot of things on mind since last weekend. For some reason, I couldn't seem to get Rodney out of my head. I decided to call Paris and see if she wanted to go get some lunch at our favorite restaurant Jino's. I made sure to call ahead of time so that our favorite booth in the back could be reserved. When we got to the restaurant, we sat down and ordered a few drinks to start off with. I sat across from Paris and just stared down at the screen of my gold iPhone 6 as it rung. It's not that I didn't want to answer it. I just didn't know what to say.

"You can answer it. I already know it's Rodney calling," Paris said. Her voice startled me from my thoughts.

I looked up at Paris with a surprised look on my face. "Huh?"

"We're twins, E. I can sense your feelings too, remember? I knew it back in the day. I just never said anything."

"How did-I mean, why didn't you ever say anything? Dang, do you know how long I've held this in? There have been so many times that I just wanted to cry on your shoulder."

"I know, I was just waiting for you to tell me yourself."

"Oh, Paris! I've missed him so much! He's my soulmate. I just know it. Yeah, he had his thugged out ways, but that's what attracted me to him in the first place; his swag, his attitude, and the way he carries himself. He's just so damn sexy to me. Ugh, I'm just so glad I can talk to you about it now," I blurted out.

"Exactly. Now you can stop holding it all in. You know you can talk to me about anything, and since when we started keeping secrets anyway?"

"I'm sorry, sis. I don't know what I was thinking. I should have said something to you."

"It's cool though, as long as you're happy. At least Rodney is a major upgrade from Peanut's punk ass. Plus, it's been a long time since I seen you smile. I was starting to get tired of them crazy ass mood swings of yours too," Paris joked, and we both burst out laughing.

"Hush, P! We can't all be like you."

"What?"

"Having a steady boyfriend and shit."

"Who, Renzo? Girl please, we are just friends. You know it's not even like that," Paris replied, rolling her eyes.

"Um huh, whatever you say. What you are doing later on?" I asked.

"Nothing, why?"

"I was wondering if you wanted to go with me to a barbecue."

"Where at?"

"Rodney texted me and asked if we wanted to come by his house later. He said he was gonna have a few friends over for a little get-together. Nothing major."

"Oh aight. Yeah, that's was sup. What time does it start?"

"He said around six, so I guess I'll go find me something cute to wear. I'll stop by later and pick you up."

"Okay cool, did you tell Ari?"

"Nah, I'm about to text her now and see if she wants to go," I said as I got up from the booth and threw two $20 bills on the table.

"Well damn, thanks for lunch sis."

"Yeah thanks my ass, you owe me."

"You know I got you," Paris said as she followed me out the restaurant.

*****

MARCUS

"Aye, chill your ass out girl. Damn, I told you I wasn't going to the barbecue tonight."

"Stop lying! I already know that's where you're going because you do whatever Rodney tells you to do."

"You don't know shit. You just assume that's where I'm going because I won't tell your nosey ass my every move."

"Why are you acting all secretive then, huh? You've been gone all damn week. Now, you're just gonna come through, scoop me up, get some of this good ass pussy and just bounce? Nah nigga, you ain't gon' treat me like a hoe."

"Monique man, calm your ratchet ass down. Ain't nobody trying to just smash and bounce. I told you the reason I'm dropping you off at home is because I got some shit to handle. Damn, you can't understand that?"

"Yea, I bet you do, but you know what? Fuck you, Marcus! I thought you promised me you were gonna take me to the mall today. You said I could get the new Jordans that just came out," Monique whined.

"Come on with all that; you know damn well it ain't gon' take all day to get no damn shoes, girl."

"Ugh! You get on my nerves."

"So what? You get on mine too. I'm getting real sick of your spoiled ass attitude. You always want me to spend my fuckin' money, buying you shit so you can stunt in front of your home girls."

"It's not like that."

"So tell me what's it like then? You don't want me to chill with my peoples because you want to spend up all my fuckin' money. You think I'm stupid?"

"Look nigga, you gon' quit talking to me like I'm a little ass girl."

"Or what? That's your problem now. You don't like when a nigga tells you about yourself."

"Shut your dumb ass up!"

"Nah, you shut the hell up with your spoiled ass."

"I'm not spoiled! I'm just used to being treated like a queen. I can't help it if I like nice shit."

"A queen? Girl please, and I saw where you grew up. Ain't shit fancy about it."

"So! That doesn't mean that I don't want nice shit now!" Monique yelled.

"Well why don't you get off your lazy ass and work for it instead of trying to take the next man's hard earned money?" I shot back.

"Cause if he's stupid enough to give it to me then I'm damn sure gonna take it."

"Oh really? That's how you feel?"

"Yes really, nigga! Ain't shit free."

"Yo, get your stanking, no good ass out my fuckin whip," I said, pulling my 2015 Tahoe on the side of the busy freeway.

"You've lost your damn mind if you think I'm getting out right here! You didn't pick me up here, so I'm damn sure not about to get out here," Monique said as she rolled her eyes and folded her arms across her chest.

"Oh, you're getting the fuck out!"

"Like I said, I'm not going anywhere until I get home, so you might as well pull on off."

"Oh, you think so? Watch this."

I got out of the truck and walked around to the passenger side door. Monique tried to hit the locks, but she was too late. I pulled the door opened and yanked her ass out of the truck.

"Move! Stop playing, Marcus! Get your hands off of me!" Monique screamed as she twisted and turned, trying to get loose from my grip.

"Nah, you got to bounce. I ain't rocking with your low down ass no more. This is it!"

"Fuck you, nigga! You wasn't shit anyway!" Monique yelled

back as she ran around to the driver side behind me. She swung over and over, hitting me in the back. Cars blew their horns as they zoomed past. I finally was able to grab the door handle and open it. I jumped into the Tahoe and tore off, leaving Monique on the side of the road looking stupid. As far as I was concerned, that bitch was dead to me.

CHAPTER 18

RODNEY

Friday Night...

I stood on the balcony of my three-story house and stared through the glass at Egypt. I knew she felt me watching her because she made sure to switch her big booty from side to side extra hard every time she walked by the glass door.

Umm, I can watch her walk all day, I thought as I turned the Corona bottle up to my mouth. I tapped on the glass with the bottle to get Egypt's attention. She looked over and saw me pointing to the empty bottle. A few minutes later, she walked over to the glass door and slid it open.

"Hey! What's up? Why you out here all by yourself at your own party?" Egypt asked as she handed me the cold bottle of beer.

"Just thinking. I like to come out here sometimes and just think."

"So, what you are thinking about so hard?"

"You," I said as I walked up behind her and wrapped my arms around her.

"Oh really? And what about me?" Egypt asked as she leaned her head back against my chest and looked into my eyes, waiting for my response.

"I was just thinking how good it is to see you again. You have no idea how much you've been on my mind. I can't thank God enough for sending you back to me. It's no coincidence that out of all the tattoo shops in Miami, you walked into mine. See, it's meant for us to be together. I'm so glad you're doing well for yourself. I worried about you, Ari and Paris every day."

"You did? Well, I can't tell. You just up and left us and never looked back. Do you know all the shit that I had to go through? I cried for you every night," Egypt said, looking down at the concrete floor.

"Nah, E. I'm sorry, baby girl. You know I would never do that to y'all on purpose. It hurt me like hell to leave y'all. I came back a few summers to check on you, but I couldn't find y'all nowhere, man. Come on now, E. Don't act like I'm some fuck nigga and ain't give a fuck. You know it broke my heart to leave you."

"Yea, well that's a long time ago, but it's good to know you at least didn't just say fuck me. I sure felt like you did, though."

"Hell no. Never. Since I got out of prison, I've been trying to change my life around."

"Say what? You were in prison?" questioned Egypt.

"Yep. I did nine out of my ten-year sentence. I got out early on parole."

"Damn, what happened? You know I would have came and saw you or wrote or something."

"It's a long story, but it's cool though. You're here now and that's all that matters. Right?"

"Right." I said as, I leaned down and kissed Egypt. It felt like fire ran through my body as she sucked on my lips. It'd been a long time since I tasted her sweet lips.

"Mmmmm," Egypt moaned.

"So how did y'all end up in Florida anyway?" I asked, breaking the kiss.

"You already know all the stuff my momma was putting Paris and I through, right?"

"Yeah."

"Well, it didn't stop. It only got worse as the years went by."

"Damn, man! That's exactly why I didn't want to leave y'all. I tried to get my pops to understand, but he thought I was just making up excuses to stay in New Jersey. Fuck!" I yelled as I banged my fist against the concrete wall.

"Calm down, Rodney; there's nothing we can do about it now. I know you tried to help us, but you were only a kid yourself. What more could you do?"

"Yeah, but I would have still blown them niggas' heads off if I would of known all the things you told me happened to you. No child should have to go to bed scared in their own home. Your mom was just sick in the head. She had no right violating you the way she did."

"Shit, who you telling? That's why we ran away."

"Damn, y'all ran away? When?"

"Hell yeah. It was about 10 years ago. Paris, Ari, and me came across a few dollars, packed our shit, and left New Jersey for good. I don't ever want to go back. It's nothing but bad memories there."

"Shit, I don't blame you one bit. It's good to see y'all again, though. It's good to see that all three of y'all stuck together after all these years. I see that booty done got all fat back there too. That nigga must be hitting it on the regular," I said, smacking her on the butt.

"Boy, you're so crazy!" Egypt giggled.

"What? You ain't deny it, so it must be true."

"Haha. Well, if you must know. No, I'm not seeing anyone. If I was, do you think I'd be out here letting you feel all on my booty? You know I don't play that."

"Ummm huh, I hear ya. So, why don't you have a man? I know these little young niggas be trying to holla at your fine ass."

"I'm serious. I'm all about my bread. I don't have time for any man.

"Oh really, so you ain't got time for me either, huh?"

"I don't know. I'll see."

"Don't get hurt, Egypt. You know you've always been my girl, and I'm not letting you go now that you're back in my life."

"And who says I'm back in your life?"

"I did. Is that a problem?"

"I don't know yet. I'll let you know. Plus, I'm still mad at you."

"I know, baby. Damn, a nigga apologized. Please forgive me," I begged.

'Nope, it's not gonna be that easy. You got a lot of making up to do, mister," Egypt pouted and poked her lips out.

"So, let me make it up then. Tell me what I've got to do?"

"I don't know yet, but I'll be sure to let you know."

"Come on E, dang. You're making me look all soft out here. I'm begging and shit."

"Ha ha, you'll be okay."

"Aye, hold on, what's going on inside?" I asked as I turned

around and looked through the glass. I could see Marcus staggering and falling into everything.

"Oh Lord, let me go see what this nigga doing before he break up all my shit."

"Yo, what the fuck! What you doing, bruh?" I yelled as I walked into the front room where Marcus had just fell into my 70-inch TV, almost knocking it on the floor.

"Aye Rodney, bruh, where you been? Come take a drink with me," Marcus slurred.

"Nah bruh, it looks like you already had too much to drink. You need to sit your ass down somewhere."

"Shit, I'm good my nigga. I'm just getting started," Marcus said, waving the bottle of Jose Cuervo in the air.

"Man, sit your drunk ass down."

"Move Rodney, I'm not in the mood to sit down. I'm celebrating, my nigga! I just left my bitch on the side of the road. You was right, bruh; that bitch wasn't shit. I should have listened to you, man," Marcus said as he pushed me in the chest and made me stumble back into Egypt, who was standing right behind me.

"Aight. Aight, come on dawg, let's go upstairs. You need to sleep it off. We can talk about it tomorrow," I told Marcus as I tried to pull him upstairs. He put up a fight, but I still managed to get him to one of the guest bedrooms.

Once we entered the room, Marcus finally gave in and stopped resisting. I turned on the light and carried him over to the bed. Marcus was so drunk that he just fell down across it. I shook my head as I snatched his sneakers off one by one and threw them on the floor. I turned the light back out and went downstairs to join the rest of my guests. Everyone partied and had a good time. Egypt, Paris, and their friend Ari were the last ones to leave. I tried to talk them into crashing in one of the guest rooms upstairs, but they insisted on driving home. I walked them out to their car because it was so late. I kissed Egypt goodnight as we stood at the back of the car. I really didn't want to let her go.

"So, when am I gonna see you again?" I asked as I held the car door for her to get in.

"Soon," Egypt replied as she climbed into the back seat of Ari's Chrysler 300 and threw her head back on the seat. I stood in my driveway and watched them drive away.

CHAPTER 19

MARISOL

Oh no his ass wasn't trying to be a gentleman and shit! He never opened doors for me. Hell, he never did anything sweet for me when we were together. I never had a choice about anything when it came to Rodney. It was his way or else, even when it came to sex. He never asked how I wanted it. He just took it whenever he felt like it. Hijo de puta! He even beat my ass if I told him no. Now, this nigga was up here opening and closing doors for bitches. I had been following his dumb ass ever since I saw him in the projects a few days ago. His punk ass had the nerve to show back up in Virginia like everything cool and shit. Little did he know, I had a surprise for his ass. If Rodney thought that he was just going to leave me to take care of his son all by myself, then he had another thing coming.

If y'all hadn't it figured it out yet, I'm Marisol, Rodney's ex. I don't play any games. Rodney may have thought he got away with the shit he put me through, but I haven't forgotten. I had to fight every day. It's like every bitch I saw wanted to beat my ass for getting Rodney locked up. I had to move out of Virginia until things cooled off, so I decided to move up north with my aunt in New Jersey. It's funny because I actually just moved back to Virginia three months ago, and guess who was the first person I saw? Rodney's punk ass. He was strolling around the block where his dad lives, like he was still running shit. I almost didn't recognize him because he'd changed so much over the years. I thought he had moved back for good until I saw him and some man that I hadn't seen before put duffle bags in the trunk. I sat in my car and waited for them to leave. I followed them all the way to Miami. I've been here a few days already, and I was following his every move.

I know y'all are like, why is she so mad? She set him up. Yeah, I got him locked away for ten years, but that didn't mean that I didn't still love him. I was just so hurt, and I couldn't believe that he beat my ass like that. To top it all off, he broke up with me just because he thought I was cheating on him. I have two little girls by Jose, my other baby daddy. That's the dude Rodney saw grabbing my ass and shit. I don't know what got into Jose. He knew I didn't want his bum ass. I guess he was just fronting in front of his little homeboy. He knew damn well that we didn't get down like that. Yeah, I used to fuck with him from time to time whenever I wanted money, but he knew it wasn't anything more than that. He got what he wanted, which was some bomb ass pussy. I got what I wanted. It was no more and no less.

I don't know what Rodney was so mad about either because he was out there doing his thing too. He acted like I was dumb or something. The only difference was that I got caught. I knew all about the little hoe that he fucked around with. I just never questioned him about it. I guess it didn't feel so good when he got beat at his own game.

I grew up poor. I only had four pairs of jeans that I washed constantly. My parents barely had enough money to feed me and my brother. We went to bed hungry almost every night. When I turned 14, I got tired of crying myself to sleep, wondering where the next meal was coming from. I started hustling nickels and dimes. It was putting food on the table, but I needed more. That's when I met a friend that introduced me to a new lifestyle. This was a lifestyle with major cash flow. All I had to do was meet up with older rich guys and listen to their sad ass sob stories about how their wives weren't pleasing them anymore. Some wanted sex, and others didn't. Either way, it didn't matter; as long as I got my paper.

I left all that alone when I met Rodney because I thought that he was my prince charming. Little did I know, he was the furthest thing from it. I wanted to show his ass who to play with, though. He was trying to skip town and shit. I knew that he heard I was pregnant while he was locked up. My cousin's baby daddy was in the same prison, and I told him to make sure to tell him personally. Obviously, that nigga could have cared less because he never even contacted me to see how the baby was doing. I knew he would be so proud of our son Jaquan. I gave him Rodney's middle name. He is only 11, but he is already above average in his class. He is very smart, and I wouldn't trade him for the world. Rodney is really missing out on getting to know a great kid. He has already missed the first 11 years of his life, but that was all about to end now. He could move to Miami and buy a quarter-million-dollar house, have two cars, and a motorcycle; yet, he never sent me a dime for his only son. I'm pretty sure he owns that tattoo shop too. *He got to be getting paid from somewhere to be living like this,* I thought as I sat across the street in my 2002 Honda Accord. I watched as all of the lights in Rodney's house went off room by room.

Hmm, I got to do some digging and find out how this nigga got out the joint and can afford to buy a crib that cost more them eight of my houses put together. I also have to do some research on the three golden girls to see why they were buzzing around my man. I took one last look at the dark house, then started my engine and pulled away from the curb.

CHAPTER 20

ARI

"Aye Kiki, do you see my phone on the kitchen table? I think I left it down there last night when I got home!"

"I don't see it!" Kiki yelled.

"Damn! Where in the hell could I have put it?" I whispered as I ran downstairs to go see if I had left it in the car. I stepped onto the hot concrete and cursed because it was so hot.

"Oooh damn! I should have slipped my shoes on," I said, as I checked everywhere in the car, but the phone was nowhere to be found.

"Ugggh! It's too damn early for this. Dang! I know I'm not crazy,"I said to Kiki as she stood in the doorway watching me. I walked across the yard to Egypt's house.

Knock. Knock.

"Who is it?"

"Ari."

Egypt opened the door and burst out laughing.

"What's so funny?"

"You, have you seen your hair? Oh my God! It's standing up

all over your head. You look like Don King," Egypt said as she burst out laughing again.

"Hush, E. I came to see if you saw where I left my phone last night. I can't find it anywhere. You know I need it for work. Can you call Rodney and see if I left it over there?"

"Hold on, hold on. Let me see…I call him real quick," Egypt said, as we walked into the living room to get her phone. She dialed the number and waited.

"He didn't answer, but I bet that's where it is."

"Damn. It probably is, but I thought I had it when I left. I can't remember. You want to go see if it's there?"

"Yea, but I ain't going anywhere with you looking like that," Egypt said, pointing at my head.

"Whatever, pick me up in ten minutes," I said as I walked out the front door and headed to my house.

*****

MARCUS

I sat up in bed and rubbed my head. Ugh, I had a major headache. Damn, my head felt like a ton of bricks were sitting on it. I rubbed my eyes, trying to adjust them to the bright sunlight shining through the crack in the curtain. I looked around and recognized the room right away. *What am I doing at Rodney's house?* I didn't usually crash here unless I was hiding out from Monique's crazy ass.

"Monique!"

Saying her name made everything from the day before start rushing back to me at once. I rubbed my forehead before I sat up to slide to the edge of the bed. I grabbed my sneakers and put them on, then I went into the bathroom to wash my face. When I opened the bathroom door, all I heard was laughing and talking, so I decided to go downstairs. I walked into the kitchen and immediately noticed the sexy chick standing at the stove. I just stared and sat down on one of the bar stools to watch her cook. *Her body is so damn sexy, and that stance is just mind blowing,* I thought, licking my lips. I couldn't help but to admire her nice round butt. She had a nigga in a daze.

"Yo nigga, you finally woke your drunk ass up!" Rodney said as he walked into the kitchen with Egypt behind him.

"Yeah bruh, and I've got a banging ass headache too."

"You should because your ass was done with last night. I swear my nigga, I had to drag your ass upstairs."

"Stop lying, nigga! I was wondering what the hell I was doing at your crib."

"I'm serious. You came up in this bitch with your own bottle, drunk as hell. I should whoop your ass for fucking up my crib last night," Rodney said, punching me on the arm.

"Nah bruh, that's my bad. You know damn well I wouldn't do some shit like that on purpose."

"Oh, you showed your ass," Ari added, sitting a plate of grits, eggs, bacon, and toast down in front of me. The smell hit my nose and instantly made my stomach growl.

"Mmm, it smells delicious. Thanks, and I apologize for my behavior last night. I was going through some things with my girl—well, my ex girl, and I let it control my way of thinking. I should have never drunk that tequila knowing I was already in a bad mood. It just made things worse. I guess I ruined your barbecue, huh bruh?"

"Nope, not really 'cause after you passed out, we kept turning up. Plus, nobody started leaving until about 3:00 a.m., and it's about damn time you get some sense and left that crazy ass girl alone. I told you she was a paper chaser," Rodney replied as he dug into the big plate of food Egypt sat down in front of him.

"Don't get used to me fixing your plate," Egypt said as she sat down next to him with her plate of food.

"Whatever girl, you know you like fixing my food."

"Uh huh, whatever boy."

"Haha, nah, but I appreciate y'all coming through and hooking breakfast up for a nigga."

"Hell yeah, I agree. I haven't had a good home cooked meal in a minute. Thank you again," I said.

"It's cool, don't mention it. So that must mean you've got the dishes then, huh?"

"Now I ain't say all of that," Rodney laughed.

"It's aight, y'all go chill. I got this, bruh; I mean, it's the least that I can do for acting an ass last night."

"I'll help you," Ari said, walking over to the sink.

"Aight, then it's settled, we got this," I said as I began raking all the leftover food into the trash can.

"Bet, well we'll be in the living room if you need us," Rodney replied as him and Egypt walked out of the kitchen.

"They look so cute together. I'm so happy my girl is finally smiling again. She hasn't actually told me yet, but I know she has feelings for Rodney that run way deeper than just friendship," Ari said as she watched them disappear around the corner.

"Hell yeah, I feel the same way about my boy. I've never seen him boo'd up before."

"Really? Wow, I can't believe that."

"Believe it; all that nigga does is work and come home. He's always told me how he felt about Egypt. I guess that's why I'm so glad they bumped back into each other after all of this time. My nigga has been through a lot, so he deserves to be happy."

"Dang, I had no idea. Even back in the day, Egypt never said anything to me about him."

I didn't respond. I just watched Ari as she let the water run in the sink. She squirted dish detergent into the water, making bubbles appear. She took her hand and moved it around in the sink to mix it all together. I leaned over her and put the empty pots in the sink. I could feel her eyes on me as I walked over and pulled the trash bag out of the can. When I walked back into the kitchen and grabbed the box of trash bags off the counter, I glanced over at the sink and caught Ari checking me out. *So, she was checking a nigga out,* I thought as I put the trash can back underneath the wooden island. I decided to see where her head was because Monique's ass was history. I needed a woman like this. I needed a woman that knew how to take care of her man.

"So where's your man at, Miss Ari? If you don't mind me asking," I said, breaking the silence.

"I don't know. If I had one, I'd be cooking him breakfast this early in the morning instead of here talking to you."

"Mm hmm, I hear ya; feisty, huh? But you've got a point. So

what's a fine woman like yourself doing single?"

"Because I don't have time for a man right now. I've got my hands full trying to raise an 11-year-old daughter that thinks she's 21."

"Oh, so you got kids?"

"Yes, one; my pride and joy, Kierra."

"That's what's up. I always wanted a little girl," I replied as I dried the last pot and put it in the cabinet.

"So, do you have any kids?"

"Nope, not yet. I guess I just haven't found the right woman to have my seed yet. I don't want to be like every other hood nigga with three and four different baby mammas. I want my child to grow up knowing mommy and daddy."

"I feel you on that. I wish every man thought like you."

"So, where's Kierra's dad? Is he still in the picture?"

"No, he was killed when I was three months pregnant with her," Ari said, looking down at the floor as she spoke.

I could sense that I had hit a soft spot, so I decided to change the subject.

"I'm sorry to hear that, ma. I didn't mean to bring up bad memories."

"It's okay."

"So, my boy told me y'all are originally from New Jersey? All y'all grew up together?"

"It's cool and nah, I saw Rodney around the hood sometimes but I didn't really know him like that. I knew Paris and Egypt since I was like 14. I think they were 12 at the time."

"Oh okay, so how long have you been in Florida?"

"Going on 12 years."

"Do you like it?"

"Yea it's cool. I miss home sometimes, but I like it. I've met some really cool people since I've been here."

"Yea, I feel you on that. I miss Jamaica so much. I want to go back and visit one day, but I'm just nervous because I haven't seen any of my family in years."

"Oh, is that where you're from?"

"Yea, originally, but my mom and I moved to the States when I was 14. I got into some trouble and got locked up. That's where I met Rodney."

"Oh wow, I've always dreamed of going to Jamaica and dang, you did time behind bars too?"

"Yea, but it was on some petty ass charges. It was stupid on my part and trust me I learned my lesson. I just chalked it up as a blessing in disguise. I was headed in the wrong direction, and I know my momma was probably cussing my ass out from heaven."

"Damn, you always gon' have a nigga hatin', no matter what you're doing. Wow, your mom passed away?" Ari asked with sadness in her voice.

"You got that right, but I'm trying to do the right thing now. Me and my nigga opened up a tattoo shop, and shit has been going good ever since. Yeah, my mom passed when I was 17."

"Sorry to hear that, and that's good shit. Y'all made a good investment. Egypt and I were just saying how we should have thought of that idea before we opened our businesses."

"Oh okay, you got your own business?"

"Yea, six actually. I'm in the process of opening my seventh one in Pamlico."

"Oh okay, what kind?"

"It's a soul food restaurant. We sell anything you can think of, from mac and cheese to fish and grits."

"Oh okay, that's what's up. What's it called?"

"Kiki's."

"Oh okay yeah, I'll have to stop by and check it out one day. I love to eat."

"Yea, you should; you won't be disappointed, I promise," Ari said, flashing me a sexy smile.

I couldn't say anything, I just smiled back at her. I admired a woman that made her own bread. It let me know that she wasn't after mine. Ari and I sat in the kitchen and talked for hours about all kinds of stuff. The more we talked, the more I was digging her. Ari was just the kind of girl that I'm looking for, so we hit it off instantly.

CHAPTER 21

RODNEY

Four Months Later...

"So when am I gonna get a chance to chill at your crib?" I asked Egypt, as I sat across the table from her and stared into those beautiful eyes of hers.

"I'm not sure yet. How do I know you're not some crazed stalker?"

"Yea, I just might be, but I promise not to hurt you unless you want me to."

"You're so silly, boy!" Egypt said, giggling.

I reached across the table and placed her hands in mine. She dropped her head and I let go of her hand. I walked around the table and stood in front of her. I lifted her chin and kissed her softly on the lips. She kissed me back with so much passion. I could feel it in every stroke of her tongue.

"Mmmmm, your mouth tastes so sweet," I said as I sucked on her bottom lip. Each time I slide my tongue out of Egypt's mouth, she let out a low, soft moan. The sound of her moaning was driving me over the edge. I put both of my hands underneath Egypt's shirt and massaged her breasts as we continued to kiss. They were much larger than I remembered, and her skin felt so soft. I couldn't take it any longer. I pulled down the white skirt Egypt had on and laid her across the patio table, then lifted her shirt over her head, exposing her large brown breasts. I started kissing all around her nipples. I licked them a few times before I put each one in my mouth and started sucking. Egypt let out a moan.

"Mmmmm, yes!" I moaned, as I sucked and flicked my tongue on her swollen nipples one at a time.

"Oooh. Yes Rodney!" Egypt purred, as I rubbed my fingers over her wet spot.

"Mmmmm, I want you so bad baby. You've kept me waiting long enough. I can't take it any longer," I said, sticking my fingers in and out of her wet tight hole.

"Stand up and turn around," I demanded in a seductive tone. Egypt did as she was told. She stood up and faced the table. I gently pushed her forward, making her lay flat on her stomach with her ass in the air.

"Damn, that ass has gotten fat as hell," I said, smacking her on the ass and making it jiggle. I got on my knees and licked her swollen love box. She moaned over and over as I licked, sucked, and teased her body. After her body couldn't take anymore, I stood up, unbuckled my jeans and placed the rubber over my nine-inch magic stick. Her juice box was dripping wet as I slowly slid inside of her.

"Oh. Yes, oh my God! It feels so good," Egypt purred.

"Umm huh, you like that?"

"Yes."

"Whose pussy is this?"

"Yours."

"Nah, whose pussy this is? I'll keep hitting it until you get it right."

"Mmm, it's Rodney's pussy, Daddy!" Egypt screamed as she released all of her juices all over me.

"Damn right it is," I replied, as I went in and out of her wetness over and over. I watched as my hard rod disappeared every time she threw her big butt back.

"Oooh girl! Damn, you about to make me tap out already. Mmm, this shit too good baby."

"Ooh yes, Daddy don't stop," Egypt moaned in that sexy voice that I loved. I couldn't take it anymore. I exploded inside of her, and luckily, I had on a rubber.

Egypt and I made love all night long. She spent the night with me for the first time in the four months that we'd been kicking it. She wanted to take things slow this time around, and I agreed because I wanted to show her that I was not the guy she thought I was. She laid peacefully in my arms all night as I watched her sleep.

It felt so good to have the woman I loved in my arms after all of this time. It felt just like old times when she would cry on my shoulders for hours until she fell asleep in my arms. She may have thought otherwise at times, but E would always have a special place in my heart.

CHAPTER 22

EGYPT

Two Weeks Later...

Knock. Knock.

"Who is it?" I yelled as I peeked through the peephole.

"I have a delivery."

"A delivery, for who?" I asked as I pulled the large door open. The sunshine felt so good against my cool cheek. "Yes, can I help you?"

"Yes, I have a delivery for Ms. Parker?"

"I'm Ms. Parker, but there must be some kind of mistake."

"Are you Egypt Parker?"

"Yes."

"Okay then, I have the right address. Could you please sign right here," the delivery guy said, handing me the small electronic device and a plastic pen.

Who in the world could have sent me flowers? It couldn't have Rodney because I had never even brought him here before, so he wouldn't even know my address. *This is kind of strange because only a few people know's that my favorite flower is a yellow rose,* I thought to myself as I sniffed the flowers and closed the door behind me. This must be some kind of joke or something.

I bet Ari told Marcus' ass how to get here, and he gave Rodney the address. I picked up my phone and shot Rodney a quick text to let him know that he was on my mind as well. I knew it had to be him who sent the flowers. He replied back with a smiley face and a kissing emoji. I smiled at the screen because I had never felt so in love until now. There had been a few times where I thought that I was, but nothing like this.

I thought I was in love with Peanut, but he only wanted me around as a punching bag. He never loved me. He just loved the fact that he could control me and if I didn't listen, he would beat my ass. I was just weak and scared, so I did everything he said to do. Never again would I let another person control my thoughts or feelings. Thank God I was strong enough to get out of that situation, and I'd never go through it again. I know Peanut was pissed when he found out that I had left town, but I didn't care. I was tired of being a sex slave for him and my momma.

Peanut had always been crazy. I remember I tried to break up with him once, and he followed me to school and hid in the girl's bathroom all day until I came in. He beat me for about 30 minutes. The only thing that made him stop was the bell ringing for lunch. He left me right there on the cold floor. That was the first time I had been hospitalized, but definitely not the last. Peanut beat me so badly that day that I had three broken ribs, a fractured arm, and a broken collar bone. Not to mention, the knots and bruises all over my body. My momma was no better because the only reason he got away with it was because they both made me lie and say I got jumped by four girls. I was so scared of getting beat like that again, so I just went along with the lie. Peanut paid her off in dope right there in my hospital room. There were just so many bad memories. I hated thinking about it, so I shook my head from side to side trying to get rid of the thoughts.

Later That Day...

I decided to go surprise Rodney at his job since he had my favorite roses delivered to me earlier today. I thought that was so sweet of him to take the time out of his day and do something special for me. I pulled into the parking lot of the tattoo shop and saw Rodney standing by his car smoking a Newport.

"Hey, baby! Why are you looking so mean?"

"Nothing bae, just motherfuckas getting on my nerves today. No biggie. Anyway, how's my wifey's day been going?" Rodney asked. He leaned through the car window and kissed me on the forehead.

"Oh, nothing new other than Kiki blowing up my phone up all day, as usual."

"Awww, she misses her Auntie."

"No, she's just trying to butter me up because she wants to go to those *Step It Up* tryouts."

"Oh yeah, I remember you telling me about that. So, you won't take her?"

"It's all the way in California and we live in Florida. Tell me how can we possibly get there and back without Ari knowing we're gone?"

"Mm hmm, you have a point but you know Ari is not going for that. Hey, you can always take me along and just say y'all are going with me on a business trip. It is summertime, you know? That means no school for the next two months. Come on, let's go! We need a vacation anyway," Rodney said.

"Okay, okay already. I've got to think of something to tell Ari first because Kiki doesn't want her to know about her trying out until she wins."

"Okay, it's all set then. When is it?"

"See, here you go spoiling her even worse than me. Ugh, I already have to hear Ari's mouth as it is. You know Kiki loves herself some Uncle Rodney. I think she said it's June 10th, which is like a month away."

"Oh yeah, that's my little partner right there, and that's what's up. That gives me plenty of time to get everything in order," Rodney said as he held the door for me to go inside the shop.

"Come on, let's go in my office. It's been a little crazy around here today. I don't want everybody all up in our conversation.

"I guess everybody's in the mood for tattoos," I joked as we walked into Rodney's huge office. It was the size of a small apartment. I was impressed as I looked around. He had a beautiful view of the ocean from his office window. It was simply amazing. I walked over and stood in front of Rodney as he sat down behind his desk. I sat on the edge of the desk, lifted both of my feet, and placed them on the arm of the chair, exposing my freshly shaven love nest. Rodney licked his lips as he watched with excitement while I unbuttoned my blouse.

"Um, hold up baby, let me lock the door."

"Ugh, hurry up," I pouted as he ran over to the door and turned the lock. I guess he didn't want to risk anyone bursting in and looking at all of my sexiness. When he turned around, I was butt naked sitting in his chair with my legs spread wide open.

"Mmmmm, damn girl. That's how you feel?"

"Come here. I've got something special in store for you," I said seductively.

"Oh yeah?"

"Yes! You surprised me earlier by having my favorite flowers delivered to my house today. So, I thought I'd surprise you by showing up to your job and rocking your world," I said, pulling his white tank top up and licking down his stomach with the tip of my tongue.

"Damn bae, that shit feels good. Mmm girl, what flowers? I didn't send any flowers," Rodney responded as he pushed her head down further on his joystick.

"The yellow roses. The ones you had delivered this morning. Dang, you need to stop smoking, boy; you can't remember nothing."

"E, I didn't send any damn flowers. I think I would remember something like that, high or not."

I stopped what I was doing and looked at Rodney like he had lost his mind. "What do you mean? Come on now bae, stop playing. Who else knows I like yellow roses, huh?"

"I don't know. All I know is that I didn't send them. You must have a secret admirer or something."

"No, I don't. You're just playing games. I know it was you who sent them."

"Aight. Keep thinking that. All I know is your ass better not have no other nigga sending you flowers and shit."

"Whatever, Rodney."

"Whatever my ass, E. You know I don't play when it comes to you," Rodney said, as he kissed me. I sat back on the desk again, spread my legs, and enjoyed the tongue fight Rodney was having with my juicy mound. *Damn, I just can't get into it,* I thought as I tried to think of who could have sent those roses. Rodney pushed deeper and deeper, making every thought in my head become a distant memory. He punished my insides until he released all his juices inside of my wetness. He didn't want to wear a rubber with me because he said he wanted his first child to be with the love of his life, which was me."

"Mmmm, that felt good baby."

"It sure was. You better get your little hot butt back to work, in here trying to seduce me," he said, fastening his jeans.

"Yeah, but you like it though, and I'm about to go because I have a client in like 20 minutes. I'll call you later," I said, kissing him on the lips before I walked out the office.

"No, call me as soon as you make it to the shop."

"Okay baby, see you later."

CHAPTER 23

EGYPT

I sat in my car and stared in the mirror as I reapplied my makeup before I met up with my next client. I put away my makeup and turned the key in the ignition, bringing the car to life. I quickly put it in reverse and proceeded to back up. A green Trailblazer cut me off doing about 40 through the parking lot.

"What's the fuckin' rush, asshole!" I yelled at the truck as it burned rubber turning out into the busy street. I shook my head as I continued to back out of the parking space. When the coast was clear, I proceeded into the heavy afternoon traffic. About a half of a mile down the street, I noticed the same car from earlier. It was parked at the little burger spot.

"Asshole! You're lucky I've got shit to do, or I would have stopped and kicked your ass!" I yelled out of the window as I rode by, honking my horn. I slowed down at the stop light, put my left signal on, and headed toward my shop. I rode in silence as I thought to myself, who in the world could have sent me those damn roses if it wasn't Rodney?

*****

PEANUT

It'd been almost 10 years since I seen my baby, Egypt. Oh my God, she's even more beautiful than the last time I saw her. I couldn't believe how much she'd grown up. I didn't mean to scare my baby when I pulled out of the parking lot behind her, but it pissed me off seeing that nigga kissing on her. Thirty minutes later, she came rushing out of the door fixing her makeup and shit. That must be the nigga who my people were telling me about. I knew damn well she hadn't been giving my pussy away. Just the thought of it made my blood boil, but I could tell by how fat that booty had grown that she had been doing something. I wanted to run up, grab that fat ass, and kiss those soft lips her when I saw her, but that little fuck boy came walking up to her. I could have easily laid his ass down right there, but I don't want it to be that easy. In due time, his ass would be mine. I don't know who that nigga was, but I didn't like the fact that he was touching on what was mine.

All of a sudden all of the loving feelings I once felt were replaced with hate and anger. It was from the thought of that nigga touching Egypt. So, she was just gonna up and leave a nigga like that without an explanation or anything, huh? I wouldn't have even known where she was if it wasn't for one of my little homie's sister, this little shawty named Marisol. She moved to Jersey a few years ago from Viriginia. She wasn't anything but a little hood hoe. Every nigga had smashed that. She came by the crib a few weeks ago crying to my little partner about how her fuck ass baby daddy had run off with some bitch and wouldn't take care of his responsibilities. Typical fuck boy. Then, the bitch got to calling names and shit, and guess whose name popped up? Yeah, you guessed it. Egypt. I knew right then that it had to be my baby.

Shawty had a sister that worked for the police department trace the tag numbers that she had written down when she tried to go and tell him about his son. Shawty said she was just curious to see who the woman was that he was with now. It didn't sound right to me, but I could care less what her fuckin' motives were, as long as she didn't fuck with my bitch. Otherwise, I'd do her worse than I'd do that nigga. He better enjoy her while he could because I was back to claim what was rightfully mine.

I hoped she liked the roses I sent to her. I even remembered that the yellow ones were her favorite kind. I still remembered everything she liked, down to her favorite color, pink. She was lucky. I could have treated her like the rest of them hoes, hit it and forget it. You know my motto, but there was something different about E. Even though she pissed me off and made me lay my hands on her, that didn't mean a nigga didn't care. I still loved her ass, no matter what. I wanted to confront her right there in the parking lot, but Marisol wanted to wait because she had something in store for her little lover boy. I was ready to crush both their hearts at the same damn time. Egypt thought she had got away, but she'd be home before she knew it.

I had something for her little sneaky ass. I'd make sure she never left again, then I'd be back to deal with her little nigga. There was no way his ass was going continue to breathe. Nobody crossed me. I only agreed to go along with this bullshit long enough to find out where my baby was. I didn't give a fuck what that bitch Marisol had planned. If she got in my way, I'd blow her fuckin' brain out too, then wait for her pussy ass brother to run up.

CHAPTER 24

PARIS

"Ugh, I'm so mad at you!" I said, taking a sip of the strawberry margarita.

"Why, what did I do?" Egypt asked with a confused look on her face.

"Because ever since you and Rodney got together, we barely get to chill anymore."

"Girl please, you know ain't nothing changed. What are you talking about? We chill all the time."

"Not like we use to E, and you know it; we used to see each other every day. Now, I'm lucky if I see you once a week."

"Haha, you need to quit Paris. You know good and well it ain't like that."

"AHEM!"

"What are you aheming for, Ari? I know you aren't talking. Ain't nobody been seeing your ass either, so spill the tea."

"Yeah, what's been keeping you so busy lately?" Egypt asked.

"Huh?" Ari replied as she leaned over the table and sucked on the straw in her cup.

"Ain't no huh, you heard what we said, Ari; don't even to play. You might as well tell it."

"Well."

"Well, what?" I snapped

"Ugh, well, I kinda met someone."

"Say what, who? When?"

"Well, y'all both know him; we are just friends at the moment because he doesn't want to rush into things, and neither do I."

"Girl, stop playing these trivia games and tell us what's really going on," Egypt said as she stuffed the last mozzarella stick in her mouth.

"Hush E and let me finish, dang! I'm surprised your big mouth hasn't told it yet. Anyway, like I was saying before I was rudely interrupted, we are just friends right now, but I think I'm starting to catch feelings for him."

"So who is he?" I asked, anxiously waiting on her to answer.

"Marcus."

"Marcus? Hold up, when did that happen?"

"Well, we've been kicking it since that morning I left my phone at Rodney's house. We got to talking and before you knew it, we just clicked."

"Wow! That's great, girl! Aww, I'm so happy for you! Now the four of us can double date. Ugggh, why didn't y'all tell me?" Egypt asked with a surprised look on my face.

"I don't know, I guess because things aren't that serious between us right now. Like I said, we are just friends." Ari said.

"Um huh, it's serious enough; y'all sure have been spending enough time together."

"I know, but Marcus and I are cool with the way things are. We just enjoy each other's company. I mean, I never wanted to be around anyone on a daily basis until I meet him," Ari replied, smiling ear to ear.

"Your ass is in love!"

"No I'm not!"

"Yes you are, I can tell from the way your face lights up every time you say his name. You haven't stopped smiling yet. It's nothing to be ashamed of. I'm glad you found somebody that you really like."

"Whatever E, I'm not in love. We're just having fun."

"Um huh, whatever you say. That nigga got a good ass job and he's sexy as hell. Girl, you better scoop his ass up before the next bitch come and takes him."

"Girl bye, that's the last thing I'm worried about. Trust me, he ain't going nowhere, boo boo. Anyway, enough about me. What's been going on with you and Rodney?"

"Nothing; I mean, things are starting to get serious. I can't believe he keeps pressuring me about moving in with him. I don't know about all that just yet. What if he starts tripping soon? Then I'll have to pack my shit."

"Why not? You know Rodney ain't gonna hurt you or let nothing happen to you. That nigga will lay in front of a moving train just to protect you."

"I know, but I just like having my own space. I'm just not ready to give up all my freedom completely and move in with him."

"You just trippin, E; you know damn well Rodney is a good man. Hell, both y'all got good niggas but you're playing. It's always a thirsty chick out there waiting on you to slip up so she can sink her claws into your meat. Y'all better listen."

"Nah, I'm like Ari, I'm not worried about a chick taking what's mine," Egypt said, waving her hand for the waitress to come over. She took our drink order and walked off, taking the empty glasses with her.

"Okay, keep thinking that. Those niggas ain't gon' wait forever on y'all asses. Y'all better get your shit together!"

"Hush, P! You don't know because you ain't got no man."

"So, that's because I don't want one right now. Trust me, I have no problem getting or keeping a nigga, sweetheart. So don't get it twisted," I snapped.

"I was just kidding, girl. Damn, chill out; don't let that alcohol go to your head. You ain't got to get all hostile on me."

"Shut up, Ari!"

"Awwww, my baby mad at me," Ari cooed as she made baby noises at me.

Egypt laughed because she knew I had a short temper. I hated when Ari called me a baby. I couldn't help it if I was the spoiled one out the crew. I guess she should blame herself. She's the one that always let me have my way. She went through hell just to make sure I didn't go without, something Nadine should have did.

"Leave me alone, Ari; ugh, you get on my last nerve always acting like a kid."

"A kid? That's you whining like a little two-year-old," Ari snapped back.

"Aight, aight, y'all chill out, we are in public if you hadn't noticed," Egypt whispered as she pointed at the other people sitting in the restaurant.

"So, fuck them! Don't nobody care because they're staring!" I yelled.

"Why do you always have to get out pocket, P? This is the exact reason I don't like going out with y'all, damn; just don't know how to act!" Egypt yelled as she got up from the table and walked to the bathroom.

Ari and I sat at the table in silence until she returned. "Aye, sis I want to apologize for the way I acted. I know you hate being embarrassed. Do you forgive me?"

"Me too, my bad E. I'm really glad we got the chance to get out and have a few drinks and I don't want to ruin it. Truce?" Ari asked as she held her hand out for Egypt to shake it.

"Truce!" we all said at the same time, making all three of us burst out laughing. We sat in the restaurant for another half hour drinking and having some much-needed girl talk. After we drank all of the margaritas we could stand, the three of us hugged and parted ways, promising to get together again soon.

CHAPTER 25

RODNEY

A Week Later...

I walked out of the jewelry store with a big smile on my face. I took my whole lunch break looking for the perfect ring for my baby. Good thing there's three jewelry stores in the same shopping center as the tattoo shop. I can't wait to see her face when I popped the question. I can see that big beautiful smile now. I'm so excited I can't hold it in any longer, I have to tell someone. Who better to tell first than my right hand man.

"Yo, Marcus! I need to holla at you for a minute!" I yelled as I walked up on the porch where Marcus was sitting.

"Aye, what's good bruh?"

"I been doing a lot of thinking lately, man."

"About what, everything cool?"

"Yeah, everything good bruh," I said, handing him the small black box. "Damn, bruh! You doing it like that? I know this shit set your ass back a little bit?" Marcus asked as he glared at the big rock.

"Hell yeah, nothing but the best for baby."

"Shit, if she say no, I'll take it," Marcus joked.

"Shut up, fool!" I said, snatching the box out his hand.

"Nah, but on the real though my nigga, she gon' love that."

"You think so?"

"Damn right. Hell, what woman you know don't like diamonds? We got to celebrate now my, nigga! Drinks on me!" Marcus yelled as he walked off into the kitchen of his three-bedroom house. It wasn't as big as mine, but it was all the room he needed for now.

"So where we going?"

"Shit, it don't matter, you tell me?"

"I'm not really feeling the club scene right now. Let's just chill and play the game, bruh. I'm trying to stay off the radar a little bit, you know, do the right thing for my bae."

"Yeah, I hear you bruh; here, try this shit right here," Marcus said, handing me the Dutch.

I took it and hit it a few times, then started coughing. "Damn! Where you get this from?" I asked as I handed it back.

"Yeah, that's some gas, huh? My little Asian partner that be coming through the shop left it for me. He be wanting me to test his shit out."

"Shit!"

"Hell yeah, and I damn sure ain't turning down no free bud," Marcus laughed.

"I know that shit right. Come on, and bring the bottles of beer so you can get your ass whooped in this new *Call of Duty.*"

"Whatever, nigga! You better catch up, I done whooped your ass three times in a row," Marcus said as he passed the Dutch back to me, grabbed the Cîroc off the kitchen counter, and walked into the front room.

We sat on the couch and played the game on his 55-inch TV. I couldn't focus because my mind kept drifting off to the perfect way to propose to Egypt. I want it to be one that she would never forget. Marcus and I decided to call it a night after we had smoked, drank, and played the Xbox until about three in the morning. Marcus beat me four times back to back. I blame it on the liquor and demand a rematch tomorrow. Marcus laughed and agreed because he knew I couldn't beat him, no matter what day it was. I have to give it to him; he was pretty good.

"Yo, call me and let me know your drunk ass made it home, man; matter fact, you need to stay here tonight."

"Nah, I'm good bruh, I'm not even drunk."

"Um huh, you say that shit all the time. You remember what happened the last time you claim you wasn't that drunk."

"Take your ass in the house, nigga. I'll hit you when I get to the crib!" Rodney yelled as I backed my car out of the driveway. As soon as I got home, I passed out on my living room couch with my phone in my hand. I was so wasted I couldn't even make it upstairs.

*****

MARISOL

So, this motherfucka thinks it's a game, huh? I know damn well he getting the messages I been sending his punk ass for about two weeks. He still hadn't responded, and I know I put my name at the end of each one, so I know he knows it's me. I got his number off his little business card. Umm huh, just as I thought; his ass did own that little tattoo shop. He must be making good money too. Shit, I was trying to get my hands on some of that. Hell, me and my son deserved to live the good life just like him.

I lost custody of my two girls to Rico's sorry ass because we had to live from place to place, and the judge felt I couldn't provide a stable home for them. The only reason I still had custody of Jaquan was because my brother was named his legal guardian by the family court judge the same day he gave my girls to Rico. Little did their dumb asses know, my brother and I lived together so I still got to be in his life full-time; what they didn't know wouldn't hurt 'em. I saw that Rodney was down here in Miami living like a damn king, I feel like his child should also. Who the

190

hell did he think he was anyway? If he could spend it on a bitch, he damn sure could spend it on a child he helped create. He might be mad at me at first, but when I put this good ass pussy on his ass, he wouldn't know what hit him. I just had to figure out a way to get that little bitch out the way; she standing in my way, and I couldn't have that. *He think he gon' give that bitch the ring that's rightfully mine, he got another thing coming,* I huffed as I peeped through the window at Rodney laying across the couch.

Peanut and I had been following Rodney and Egypt's every move for the last two weeks. I wanted to wait until the right time before I crushed their worlds, but Peanut couldn't wait another second to get Egypt away from Rodney and back into his arms. He told me that every time he thought of him going inside of Egypt, it made him want to blow Rodney's brains out. I didn't know what was so special about her ass, but like I told that nigga on the ride down here, he better not lay a finger on Rodney. He just don't know, I feel the same way about Rodney as he do about his little bitch.

"Yo, it's almost time," I spoke into the phone, then ended the call just as quickly as I made it. I ran back over to my car, making sure no one saw me as I jumped in and sped away.

CHAPTER 26

RODNEY

I was glad this day is finally over; now I could go home and take a long hot shower, then hit Egypt up to see if she wanted to come over and chill. *I still haven't figured out a way to ask her to marry me yet, I* thought as I installed the new tattoo machine in the last booth. I turned my head toward the front door when he heard the bell ringing, indicating someone had come in.

"Sorry, we're closed!" I yelled. After about two minutes, I still didn't hear the bell go off, letting me know that whoever came in had left.

"Damn! I don't know why Marcus ass ain't lock the door after he left," I mumbled as I got up and walked into the front lobby area. As soon as I turned the corner, I stopped in my tracks. I just stood there and stared at the figure standing in front of me.

"Wh—"

"What am I doing here? Well, since you seem to be avoiding my calls and text messages, I thought I would pop up and surprise you in person," Marisol said as she stood by the receptionist desk with her hands on her hip.

"Yea, I saw 'em. So what? How you get my number anyway, and why you checking up on me all of a sudden, looking me up and shit? Shouldn't you be somewhere living it up off my fuckin bread?" I yelled, making Marisol back up a little bit.

"Oh Rodney, I've missed you so much," Marisol said, trying to avoid my questions as she walked closer and tried to hug me, but I pushed her away.

"Go on with all that shit, girl."

"What's your problem? I know you ain't still mad about some stupid ass shit that happened ten years ago!"

"It's been almost 12, to be exact, and you damn right I'm still mad, bitch! I spent nine years in prison all because of your hoe ass. Do you know what the fuck that feel like? Huh?"

"Rodney, calm down baby."

"Ain't no calm down, and you been lost the privilege to call me baby. Don't ever say that shit to me again. Matter of fact, what you come here for? What did you expect me to do? Throw you a fuckin' welcome party, bitch? I ain't glad to see your stanking, trifling, back stabbing, grimy ass!" I yelled as I turned to walk away, but Marisol grabbed me by the arm, stopping me.

"You might not be happy to see me now, but you'll be begging for mercy when I put your sorry ass on child support!" Marisol shot back.

I froze as soon as the words left her mouth. "What the fuck you talking about? Child support?"

"Yeah, don't stand there and act like you don't know I had your son. You think you hate me now, but you just wait though!"

"Girl, chill with all that bullshit. What you mean you had my son?"

"I thought you knew."

"How the hell I'ma know when my ass been locked the fuck up for nine years Marisol?"

"Well, I sent word to you in there. I even wrote you a few times myself, but you never responded."

"Hell nah, I threw every letter you sent me in the trash. I wasn't trying to hear shit you had to say."

"Well, I had a son that I named Jaquan."

"Ja'Quan, huh? Damn, this shit is crazy. Why now though?"

Yes, Ja'Quan Marquise. I would have been told your ass if I would have known where you was at after you got out."

Damn, what I'm gon' do now? I'm about to get engaged and marry the woman of my dreams, then my ex shows up a drops a fuckin' bombshell on my ass, I thought as I continued to pace the floor, trying to focus on everything Marisol was telling me. She was steady talking going on and on, but all her words went unheard.

"So, how I know he's mine? You never answered my fuckin' question. I asked you how the hell you find me?"

"What you mean, nigga?"

"You heard me. How the fuck do I know he's mine? You know your ass was fucking any nigga with a bankroll. Don't even play with me."

"Whatever, Rodney. I knew you were gonna question if he was really yours, so I'm not denying you a blood test. If you feel that will make you love him more, then by all means we can get one. To answer your dumb ass question, I was visiting family down here and we dropped by your little club one night. You didn't see me, but I saw you so I asked the bartender who you were, and he said you owned the place.

That damn Leroy. I see I have to remind him how to keep his mouth shut when it came to me. As far as he know, she could have been a damn cop. *Mr. B is gonna have to check his dry snitching ass boy.*

"Damn right I want one, just for my peace of mind. I'm not tryin' to be taking care of another nigga's seed. Who the hell you think I am? You show back up after all of this time claiming your son is mine and you think I'm not gonna question it? Girl, you must have lost your mind! You played me once, but you won't do it again."

"Anyway, I have more important stuff to do than argue with you. Whenever you ready to take that test, hit me up. As a matter of fact, I have your number, I'll be in touch," Marisol said as she turned and walked out the door, making sure to switch her big butt extra hard; she knew I was looking.

She left out as quietly as she entered, leaving me speechless. I licked my lips as I stood in the door and watched Marisol's big butt bounce up and down as she walked across the street.

"Umm, that don't make no sense," I whispered to himself. I know she has something up her sleeve. I'd never seen her ghetto ass handle any situation this calm.

CHAPTER 27

EGYPT

Three Weeks Later...

"Oh my God! California is so beautiful! Auntie Egypt, can we please move out here," Kiki begged.

"What you think Ari gonna say about that? I don't think she'll like that too much."

"Well, we don't have to tell her."

"Ha ha, she do have a point," Rodney responded.

"You hush, don't go encouraging her any further."

"So, what time are we going to the beach? Ooh, I can't wait to go shopping. Oooh, all my friends are gonna hate on me when they find out my clothes came all the way from California."

"Aye, slow down little lady, you might want to catch your breath first. We just got here a few hours ago; let's get some rest. It's only 9 o'clock in the morning, and then we can go sightseeing later. You better be trying to rest up for the auditions tomorrow anyway."

"I'm ready, Auntie. I'm too excited to rest."

"Well, how about at least try to get a little bit, deal?"

"Okay. Ugh!" Kiki huffed as she dropped her luggage on the bed. She pushed the purple ear buds into her ear and fell face first onto the bed.

"Ugh, kids," I mumbled as I walked out of the room where Kiki was and went back into the adjoining room with Rodney. I unzipped my bag and unpacked my clothes, putting them in to the empty dresser drawers. We had reservations for a whole week, so I figured I may as well get comfortable.

Ari had no clue we were all the way in Cali. She thought we rode to Atlanta with Rodney to look at a new business location. She agreed for Kiki to go with no hesitation. I was surprised at first seeing as she was so overprotective of her. I knew she would have a fit if she knew where we really were at. I mean, I knew she trusted me with her but Ari was crazy over Kiki, and her being this far away from home without her permission would make Ari's ass have a heart attack.

"Come here, baby," Rodney said, pulling me down on the by my arm.

"What's up, bae?"

"I was thinking later tonight, we can go have a drink or something, just you and me. I mean, after Kiki goes to sleep, of course."

"Well, that's fine with me and we don't have to worry about

Kiki. She gonna be so worn out she ain't gon' want to do nothing but sleep anyway."

"Ha ha, smart, real smart."

"Yep, I bought her here in one piece, and I plan on returning her the same way."

"I know that's right, that's how I feel about your sexy ass. I'll protect you with my life. That's why I hate for you to be living in big house all by yourself. You never know what a crazy person might try to do."

"I'm fine, Rodney. I told you, I've got to think on it. I been living in my house this long by myself and nothing has happened; plus, I got nosey neighbors that watch everything," I joked.

"Well, I still don't like it," Rodney said, kissing me on the neck.

"Mmmmm, you better stop! You know that's my spot," I moaned softly.

"Don't worry, we'll finish this later," he said, smacking me on the butt.

"See, you play too much! You lucky I can't do what I want to do to you right now."

"Um hmm, I hear ya. Come on, let's get a few hours of sleep so we can get up and see what Cali got to offer. I always wanted to come out here."

'Yes, I have too," Rodney said as he laid on his side and held me tight in his arms. We pillowed talked for a few more minutes until we both drifted off to sleep.

*****

Five Hours Later...

Auntie E? Wake up! Wake up, you gonna miss all the fun!" Kiki yelled, shaking me on the shoulder and trying to wake her up.

"Mmmm, I'm up; what is it, Kiki?"

"Get up! You're gonna sleep all day? Uncle Rodney and I done been out shopping and everything."

I sat up in the bed and rubbed my eyes, trying to wake up. "Where y'all been?"

"We went everywhere! Uncle Rodney is the best! Look at all the stuff he bought me!" Kiki yelled excitedly, pulling outfit after outfit out of the shopping bags.

"Why didn't y'all wake me up, and where my stuff at?"

"We tried."

"Yep, we sure did; here, this is yours. I hope you like it because I'm not really used to picking out girl stuff," Rodney said, handing me the pink shopping bag. I quickly grabbed the bag and dug inside to see what I had. A big smile spread across my face when I pulled the hot pink Michael Kors purse out the bag.

"Oh my goodness! Thank you, baby! Oh yeah, I been wanting this bag for the longest. Awww, you're the best bae!" I screamed as I kissed him on the cheek.

"See, I told you he the best," Kiki said, making Rodney and I burst out laughing.

"Hush girl, and go put your things away. What time is it?"

"Almost 5 o'clock."

"Dang, that plane ride wore me out. I can't believe I slept so long. Woooh, it' been a long time since I've been able to sleep this long," I said, stretching.

"You was looking so peaceful. I didn't want to wake you. Trust me, I hated to leave your sexy ass in bed all alone."

"So why did you?"

"Because I had to take my niece shopping."

"Um huh, well Auntie want to go shopping too," I joked.

"You know you can get anything you want. Matter of fact, go take a shower and get dressed. We got dinner reservations at The Belvedere restaurant for 7 tonight. One of the finest restaurants in Beverly Hills. I have a homeboy that hooked me up on it."

"Oooh okay, look at you; doing it big in Cali, huh?"

"Ha ha, nah; just enjoying this much-needed vacation."

"So, what about Kiki?"

"Kiki and I have an understanding. She went shopping today, and tonight you and I get to go on our date."

"Sneaky little devil," I laughed as I walked off into the bathroom.

CHAPTER 28

RODNEY

Egypt and I walked into the luxurious five-star restaurant. The waiter found our names on the guest list and showed us to our table. The restaurant looked amazing; it looked like something off the *Titanic*. Each table had a white cloth draped over it with crystal champagne glasses by each plate. Every table was decorated with a big bouquet of red roses in the center, and each table looked exactly the same; it was just breathtaking.

"Wow, baby! This looks simply amazing," Egypt whispered as I pulled the chair out for her to take a seat.

"I was thinking the same thing. I can't believe how beautiful it is; my home boy told me I was going to be impressed, but damn, I had no idea it was gonna look like this."

"Awww, I love it baby. I've never seen anything so beautiful in my life."

"Neither have I bae, but I want to experience this kinda stuff with you. I want to see you smile like this for the rest of my life," I said as I reached out and grabbed Egypt's hand.

"Yesss, I wouldn't mind eating like this every night."

"Nah, you not hearing me, E. This is just a token of my love for you. You deserve the best, and I want to make you happy for as long as I live."

"You do make me happy, Rodney; you always have. What do you mean?"

I dug into my pocket and pulled the small black box out as I stood up. I walked around to Egypt and took her hand as I bent down on one knee. I looked her in the eyes as she opened the box. Egypt's eyes got big when she saw the huge rock blinging.

"Aaaaaahhh! Rodney! Yes!"

"Hold up baby, chill out for a sec; let me ask you first."

"Okay, okay. Oh my God! I can't believe it."

"Believe it, baby. Now, to my best friend, my soulmate. I want you to know that you have always meant the world to me. Even when we were kids, I knew it was you that I wanted to spend the rest of my life with. I know we've been apart for quite some time, but I want you to know there's never been a day that I wasn't thinking of you. So with this ring, I promise to love and cherish you for the rest of our lives if you let me. Will you marry me, Egypt Parker?"

"Yessss! Yessss!" Egypt yelled.

"Hold still bae, let me put it on your finger."

"I'm trying to, boo. I'm just so nervous, I don't know what to do. It's so gorgeous, I LOVE YOU, RODNEY."

"Awwww, I love you too baby, and I love to see you smile. I want to be the reason you smile daily. I don't ever want to see you hurting," I said, kissing her lips as she stuck her tongue inside my mouth and kissed me back.

We spent the rest of the night being chauffeured around California. It was even more beautiful at night. Egypt almost lost her mind when I told the driver to take us over to the Golden Gate Bridge. She snapped pictures the entire bridge ride, some of me and her, but mostly of the scenery outside the window. Her eyes lit up like a kid in a candy store.

"Damn," I mumbled to myself when I felt my phone vibrating in his pocket. I quickly pulled it out and turned it off 'cause I know it was nobody but Marisol calling for the tenth time. I gave Kiki the limo number in case she needed us, so I don't know why I was even worrying about that phone right now. My plan was to tune everybody out and enjoy the evening with my fiancée, and that's just what I was gonna do. *Without any distractions,* I thought as I leaned over and put my arms around her waist, watching as she snapped pictures of everything that passed by.

Marisol might think she's crazy, but she ain't seen nothing yet. Egypt's ass was beyond crazy, and that temper was even worse. I told her ass to stop calling and texting me. She didn't know I had a girl, but I still don't want her calling my phone. I told her stupid ass I'd hit her up when I get back in town so we could get that test done. She claimed she was gonna bring Ja'Quan to Florida to let me meet him after the test results come back, but like I had told her before, I wasn't trying to get attached to him before I know the truth. What if it turned out that he was not even mine? I mean hell, I had feelings too, so it would not have been fair to either one of us. Why put a child through that kind of trauma if the test turned out negative?

Egypt and I went back to our hotel room after about four hours of just riding around and making love in the back seat of the limo. I went straight to Kiki's room door and unlocked it. I peeped my head inside and saw her stretched out with her mouth wide open, snoring. I closed the door back and locked it, then I went inside the bathroom and joined Egypt in the shower. I made sweet love to her for hours under the hot steaming water.

The next day, Egypt couldn't wait to wake up and tell Kiki the big news. Kiki was more excited than she was. They didn't waste any time hopping on FaceTime with Paris and Ari to share it with them. All you could hear was screaming, talking, and then more screaming. I couldn't take it any longer, so I told Egypt I'd go get us some breakfast. I had to get out of that room fast. I grabbed my phone out the jeans I took off last night and walked out the door. As soon as I turned it on, the first thing I saw was 20 text messages, all from Marisol's crazy ass. I clicked on them to see what crazy shit she was talking about now. I had told her that I was not fuckin' with her like that anymore. She just couldn't get it through her head.

I clicked the first message, which was a picture message. I waited for it to download. Once the picture popped up, my heart sunk to the floor as I stared at the little boy. He had the biggest brightest smile with a head full of curly hair that was cut short. He looked just like me, except for the green eyes that he got from Marisol. All kinds of thoughts and feelings came rushing to me at once.

When I opened the next picture, I saw that she had labeled it YOUR FAMILY. It was a picture of her and Jaquan at the park. Deep down in my heart, I knew he was my son. I hated to question him, but Marisol left me no choice. What was a nigga supposed to think when he caught your ass cheating already? I shot Marisol a quick text letting her know I wanted to get that test done as soon I got back in town. She replied back fast as hell with heart and smiley face emojis. I didn't respond back. I just stuck the phone back into my pocket and went outside to the hotel lobby to find a cab so I could go get breakfast.

It didn't take long to pick up the food and get back to the room. When I got inside, I could still hear Egypt and Kiki on the phone talking and laughing. They were already making plans and picking out dates. I just set back and ate my food as I listened to them go on and on about cakes and bridesmaid dresses. The rest of the trip went as planned. We enjoyed ourselves and everything was perfect. I think we visited every spot we could in a week's time. Kiki made it to her audition, and she killed it. She was a really good dancer and over time, she'd only get better. I told her when we got back to Miami that I would pay for her to get the best dance coach money could buy.

Our trip turned out great and I hated for it to end. That meant no more holding my baby all night while she slept. I was getting used to opening my eyes every morning and seeing her. I mean, don't get me wrong, Egypt spent a few nights with me at my crib, but it was different being able to see her every day. When she spent the night, either I was rushing off to work or she was. That's why I stayed on her about moving in with a nigga. Damn, she acted like she was scared to stay under the same roof as me or something. I don't know what it was, but I just wished she would stop playing and move on in. She couldn't say no forever, and I surely hoped she didn't think we were going to be living in separate houses once we get married. That shit wasn't happening.

CHAPTER 29

ARI

Once the car came to a complete stop, Kiki jumped out, ran up to me, and gave me the tightest hug she could. She almost knocked me on the ground.

"Well, I'll have to send you off more often. I see you come back giving out hugs."

"No, Mommy. I just missed you, that's all."

"Hmm, I can't believe that. Since when did you start missing me? What did you do to my child, and where can I get another one?" I asked as I hugged Egypt.

"Whatever ma, you know you missed me too. You just tryin' to flex," Kiki said, carrying her bags into the house.

"Girl, I done told you about your mouth. Keep on now! That child learn a new word every day, I swear."

Egypt just laughed as she followed me in the house with the rest of Kiki's stuff. Kiki came running downstairs with a handful of papers. She handed them to me while she and Egypt stood quietly as I read them.

"What's this?"

"It's my contract, Momma, I wa—"

"I'm not blind. I know what it is, I can read. The question is, why am I just now hearing about this?"

"I didn't want to ruin the surprise."

"Ain't no surprise, and it ain't gon' be no show if I say you're not doing it."

"Momma! Why not?"

"Because I sa—"

"Ugh, why do you always do this? I can't ever do anything! All you want me to do is sit in this stupid house all day!" Kiki yelled before running upstairs.

"Hold on now, Ari. You being unreasonable right now. Why are you treating her like that?" Egypt said.

"I'm not being unreasonable! She should have asked me instead of trying to do shit all sneaky. What are you tryin' to defend her for? It's not like you mentioned it either. You took my child somewhere without my permission! What if something would have happened? You left me under the assumption that y'all were in Atlanta. Not halfway across the fucking country!"

"Whatever, Ari. I've had a long ass plane ride and an even longer morning, so don't come at me like I'm your child or something. Since when have I ever let anything happen to Kiki? What you need to do is stop acting like my no good ass momma and learn to be more supportive when your child wants to do shit you should be proud of! Instead of always making her feel like you're never there for her. No wonder she don't tell you shit! I'm not in the mood for your attitude today. I swear it's too early for this shit," Egypt said, walking out the door to her car.

I stood on the porch and looked as Egypt backed out of the driveway and pulled into her garage across the street. The words cut me deep like a knife. I couldn't say anything because Egypt was completely right. I thought hard about how I had just acted.

"Damn, I can't believe I'm treating my baby like that," I mumbled as I walked inside the house and went upstairs to Kiki's room. I tapped on the door a few times before she finally answered.

"Come in."

"What you doing?" I asked as I opened the door and walked inside her bedroom.

"Nothing, just listening to my new CD Uncle Rodney got me."

"Oh okay, so how did you like the trip, did you enjoy yourself?" Kiki didn't answer; she just looked up at me with a confused look on her face. I guess it felt weird that I was actually having a conversation with her instead of fussing.

"Look baby girl, I know that I haven't been the best mom that

I should have been to you lately. I promise you, I never want you to feel like I don't love you. You're everything to me. Without you, I don't know where I would be right now. Becoming a mother was the best thing that ever happened to me. It changed my life, and I'm truly sorry for how I been acting toward you lately. It's no excuse, and I understand if you hate me," I said, as tears started to roll down my cheek. I tried to wipe them away before Kiki saw them, but it was too late.

"No Mommy, I don't hate you, please don't cry. I love you with all my heart," Kiki replied as she wiped my tears away.

"Awww, I love you too baby girl. You don't know how happy it makes me feel to hear you say that, and I want you to know I'm very proud of you. My baby girl is gonna be a superstar," I managed to joke as she continued to wipe my eyes.

"Yes! Oh my God, I can't believe it. I couldn't wait to get home so I could tell you the good news. I didn't want to tell you until I made it. Then after I auditioned and got the spot, I just wanted to surprise you. I'm sorry for not telling you Mommy, and please don't be mad at Auntie Egypt. The only reason she didn't tell you is because I begged her not to. I don't want y'all fighting because of me."

"It's okay. I know you were in great hands. I just overreacted. I'll be sure to call E later so we can talk. Yes, my baby 'bout to be on *Step It Up*. The hottest teen show out right now. I'm telling everybody I know."

"You so silly, Momma," Kiki said as she laid her head on my shoulder. I sat on the bed and listened while Kiki talked about everything they did in California. Afterward, I went downstairs and made lunch for us. The rest of the day went by smoothly without any fussing or debating out of Kiki. I kind of liked the little talk that we had. I learned a lot of things about of her that I can't believe I never knew. I told her that we were gonna sit down at least once a week and talk about anything on her mind. I just wanted her to feel like she could come to me about anything, no matter how she think I'm gonna react.

I wanted to have that mother and daughter relationship that my mom and I never got a chance to have. I wanted her to have everything I didn't. That's why I worked so hard to maintain the type of lifestyle that wasn't offered to me. I was trying to teach her that nothing in life was easy. You had to work for what you wanted. That was a one in a million chance that me, Egypt, and Paris got. I just looked at it as God's way of looking out for us. My grandma always had this saying, "*He ain't go put no more on you than you can stand,*" and I truly believed that.

My mind suddenly drifted off to my grandmother. I hadn't spoken to her in 11 years. I missed her so much. Oh, what I wouldn't give for one of those big hugs of hers. I knew she was still mad at me for not coming back home, but what did I look like going back to the slums when I was living like a queen down here? I wished I could get her to move down here. I even promised her I'd buy her a new house and all, but she just wouldn't leave New Jersey. I had a friend that kept an eye on them for me, and he told me that my little brothers finally talked her into moving out of the projects, but I knew there was no talking her into leaving Jersey altogether.

I recently reached out to my brothers through Facebook. I hadn't seen them in person yet, but we talked on the phone all the time. I was thinking about taking a trip up there soon to visit, but I didn't know yet. I had to see how the girls felt about that.

Kiki was in her room doing God knows what, so I just sat back with a glass of wine and texted Marcus for the rest of the night. I also shot Egypt a quick text thanking her for everything she did for Kiki, and apologized about snapping at her earlier. She replied back; *love you sis...anytime.* I just smiled at the phone because I knew my girl wouldn't be trippin' over something so petty. That's what I loved about our bond. We were sisters no matter how mad we got at each other. We always apologized, and we never stayed mad at each other for long.

CHAPTER 30

RODNEY

I sat on the beach and watched how the waves rose high, and then came crashing back down into the ocean. No matter how high or big the wave got, gravity still brought it back down. That's how my life felt right now. It was as if it didn't matter how much I tried to do the right thing; something always came crashing down as soon as I was at my peak. I didn't know what to do right now, and I couldn't believe that I was a father. I got the test results in the mail today. I didn't know how to feel about all this. I was happy about my seed, but I just didn't know how E was going to take me just popping up out of nowhere with a 12-year-old son. I knew she going to be all in her feelings because she wanted to have my first child.

Then, I had Marisol in my ear trying to get all in my head. Her ass had been blowing my phone up all day. I guess she thought because the test came back positive that I was going to jump up and take her ass back, but it wasn't that easy. At one point, I did want to settle down and start a family with her, but after she did that fuck shit to me, there was no way I could trust her ass anymore. I hated that I didn't get in touch with her sooner.

I lied when I told I her that I didn't know she was pregnant. Yeah, I knew. Her little messenger boy got a swift ass-kicking behind that shit too. At that time, I was young and dumb. I didn't give a fuck and felt like that bitch had already betrayed me in the worst way, then she wanted to send word through her fuck ass people that she was pregnant with my seed? I beat that nigga so bad that he had to be moved to another prison. I guess I whooped his ass so bad that he was too scared to even mention it to Marisol. I didn't think her ass was really pregnant anyway, so I never thought about the shit anymore until she showed up a few months ago.

"Damn, if this girl don't stop calling my phone. Ugh, every five minutes," I said, looking at the phone as Marisol's name flashed across the screen.

"Yo, what's good?"

"Nothing, what you doing?"

"Why? What do you want, girl?"

"Dang! I was just calling to see what my baby daddy was up to, but I guess you around one of ya little bitches or something."

"Aye, chill with all that dumb shit, man. What do you keep blowing my jack up for? I know damn well you ain't been calling every five minutes just to see what I'm doing."

"Well, actually, I called to see when you wanted to meet your son. I was thinking about brin—"

"Yo, when I'm ready, I'll let you know. I got a lot going on right now and I don't need you in my ear pressuring me and shit!"

"I wasn't pressuring you, I was just asking you a question. Why you got to be so nasty?"

"Because man, you just come drop this shit on me out of nowhere. What did you expect me to do? I already got my own shit going on. You just want me stop my life and cater to your ass."

"No I don't, Rodney. The only thing I want is for you to spend time and get to know your child. Your only son. Is that too much to ask?"

"Yeah, aight. Where are you at anyway?"

"At my hotel room, but I'm about to get ready to pack up and go. I guess I got what I came for, right?"

"What's the address? Matter of fact, text it to me. I'm about to drop a few dollars off so you can take my son somewhere nice when you get home."

Marisol texted the hotel address and room number to my phone as soon as I hung up. I typed it into my GPS and saw that it was only ten minutes away in the opposite direction, so I whipped around on the highway and headed toward the hotel.

CHAPTER 31

MARCUS

One Month Later...

"So, what time you planning on showing up at the church for Rodney and Egypt's wedding rehearsal? You know they want everyone to be there early."

"I don't know yet. I've got to stop by the shop and check on a few things first, then I'll be there. You know I wouldn't miss it for the world," I replied as I stood in front of the mirror and adjusted the collar of my shirt. Ari walked up behind me, wrapped her arms around my waist, and laid her head against my back.

Mmmmm, I love the way she touched me. She turned me on in so many ways. I mean, a nigga wasn't in love or anything like that, but I did like her a lot. I wasn't trying to get married and be on that cuddling up type of shit like Rodney's crazy ass. I liked to hit and dip. I'd spend a few dollars on a chick if she was giving up that cake. Call me what you want, but I wasn't looking for any damn love. I liked things just how they were. I feel like people just loved you until you no longer served a purpose for them anymore. Then bam! Just like that, the love is gone! Look how Monique's trifling ass tried to do me. I let my guard down just for a second, and she tried to play a nigga. I knew all women weren't the same, but I still wasn't going to keep opening my heart up for it to be crushed all over again. Nah, I'd pass on that. Why go and change things up by adding labels? It only made shit complicated when we were just having fun. Ari already knew how I felt. I thought she was on the same level as me until she started getting all clingy. Now, she wanted to lay up under a nigga and shit. I wasn't with all of that. I noticed that she didn't start acting like that until after she spent a week with me. Kiki had gone to California with Egypt and Rodney on vacation. I cared about Ari, but I wasn't trying to fall in love.

"Ummmm, I just love holding you in my arms. I hate to let you go! Why do you have to leave?" Ari pleaded, squeezing me tighter.

"Come on with all that, ma; you know I've got to go to work. You know how we roll. So why you trying to change things up?" I asked as I pushed her hands away from me and walked over to the dresser to slide my sneakers on. Ari walked over and stood in the doorway, and stretched her arms out to keep me from leaving.

"Move out the way, man! You already know I got shit to do."

"Hell nah, nigga. You think you're gon' just keep coming up in my house, fucking me whenever you want to, and then just bouncing?"

"Why do you have to make stuff complicated, Ari? Damn! Why can't you just be fuckin' happy with the way things are? You get what the fuck you want from me, right?"

"Yeah but—"

"Ain't no but's; yeah, I come through but I fuck your little ass good, don't I? I buy you whatever you want, but your nut ass still has to question shit."

"Yeah, but I make my own money, Marcus. I don't need you to buy me shit."

"So what are you complaining for?"

"I want more, Marcus."

"Oh my God. Here we go. More, like what Ari, huh?"

"I want a man that I can wake up to every morning. I want to know that he's coming back home to me at the end of the day. I want a man to look at me for more than just a piece of ass. Why can't I find true love, huh? Why can't anyone love me?" Ari cried as she dropped her arms and slid down onto the floor with her back against the wall.

"Damn Ari, I apologize. I never meant to make you cry. That's the last thing I would ever try to do. Shit, I thought you enjoyed the way things were going between us," I said as I wiped the tears from her cheek.

"I did. I mean I do, but I just want to feel like I'm special to someone other than Kiki and my sisters. I know they love me unconditionally, but it's not enough. I just want to find the right man that feels the same way about me as I do about him. I want a relationship. I'm tired of being someone's girlfriend. I want to have a husband one day too. It's not like I'm getting any younger. I can't help but wonder when I'll meet my prince charming."

Ari cried harder as I wiped the tears from her eyes. It made me feel like a kid again. It brought back the memories of when I used to catch my mom crying in the middle of the night. She would be in her bedroom with the door cracked, and I could hear her crying her heart out for hours. She would tell me what made her so sad, and I never questioned it. I would just lay her head on my small shoulder and console my mom as I wiped her tears away. I knew most of her pain came from being in a new place where she barely could provide for us. I hated to see my mom cry, and I promised she would never have to cry again. I held my word up until the day she died. It made me happy to know that she died proud of me. She never knew about any of the things I did out in the streets to put food on the table for us until she met my stepdad.

"Come on bae, let's get up off this floor," I said as I scooped her up into my arms like she was a newborn baby. I carried her over to the bed and laid her down. She balled up in a fetal position and continued to cry.

I knew that I talked a lot of tough shit, but a nigga had a heart. I curled up behind her on the bed and wrapped my arms around her waist. Her sobs tugged at my heart like a guitar string. At that very moment, I felt something for her that I was trying to deny the entire time. I never had a girl cry over me before, so she had me all my feelings. I didn't know what to do to make the situation better, so I softly kissed her on the neck as I pulled her closer to me. I did the only thing I knew that would take her away from all the pain she was feeling inside. I started sucking on her earlobe. Ari's sobs slowed down and she loosened up in my arms. I started licking all over her neck as she wiped her tears away. Ari kissed me back as I planted wet, juicy kisses on her lips. She sucked on my tongue as I moved in and out of her warm mouth.

"Marcus I—"

"Shh," I whispered as I turned her onto her back and straddled my legs around her soft thighs. I leaned over and kissed in between her big breasts, and made a trail with my tongue down to her belly button.

"Mmmm," Ari moaned.

I continued to lick her body until I reached her sweet spot. I took the tip of my tongue and flicked it around in her wetness, making Ari's legs shake uncontrollably. I kept teasing her juice box until she was hanging off of the bed trying to get away from me.

"Where are you going? Don't try to run," I said as I slid her to the edge of the bed and started drilling my thick meat inside of her.

She looked even more radiant as the sunlight danced off her sexy body. I admired her sexy ass skin tone against mine. Ari dug her nails into my back as I pushed deeper and deeper inside of her. She kissed me wildly all over my face and neck.

"Oh baby, damn; mmm, that shit is turning me on."

"Oh yes, Daddy; that's what I'm trying to do," Ari purred as she sucked on my earlobe.

"Hell yeah, just like that bae! Mmmm mmmmm!"

"Yes, right there baby. Oh, give it to me!" Ari screamed out in pleasure as I flipped her over.

"Damn right, throw that shit back baby! Mmmmm, I love you!"

"I love you too," Ari purred as she looked back at me and smiled. I didn't stop. I just kept my pace until it felt like I was about to explode. That's when I pulled out of her and let all my juices go on her big round butt while she made her cheeks bounce up and down.

After I finished laying it down on Ari's ass, I decided to hit Rodney up and let him know I wasn't coming in today. I wanted to spend the day with Ari. I must have put it on her ass because she fell asleep in my arms as soon we laid down. I couldn't front, though; as I lay in her bed and flipped through the channels of her

60-inch flat screen TV, I had to admit I could get used to this. Nothing good was on, so I sat back and let my mind wander. I thought about the three magic words I said to Ari just a few minutes ago. It wasn't that I didn't mean it. It's just I couldn't believe it actually slipped out. We stayed in bed all day until it was time to head to the church for Egypt's and Rodney's wedding rehearsal.

CHAPTER 32

ARI

The wedding rehearsal at the church went well. Everyone decided to go to Egypt's house for the rehearsal dinner. The wedding was two weeks away, so everything had to be in order by the time they said "I do."

I had a big surprise in store for everyone. This would be the best wedding gift Egypt could ever get. I couldn't wait to see the look on her and Paris' face when they saw my special guest. The only person who knew about it was Marcus. He helped me mastermind the entire thing once I explained most of the situation to him about running away from my family. I told him how I had recently gotten in contact with my two brothers through Facebook. I was planning on taking a trip to Camden, New Jersey to see them, but I figured this way would be a whole lot better. Plus, I wouldn't have to hear Egypt's mouth about not going back up there. I did manage to get my brothers to agree on a two-week vacation here in Miami. I figured why not surprise everyone at dinner tonight. I couldn't wait to see them. Oh my God, so many years had passed. My stomach was in knots waiting on them to arrive. I tried to get Grandma to come but as usual, she wouldn't budge.

"Jashan just called. He should be pulling up any minute, and Mikey hasn't replied to any of my texts. I talked to him last night though, and he said that he should be getting here around 2:45 p.m.," Marcus whispered in my ear.

"Well, Jashan better hurry up because he was supposed to be at the church earlier. Ugh, he know I told him last night that I needed his help for the next couple of weeks," I snapped as I placed the silverware neatly on each place mat.

"You know he'll be here. Stop worrying yourself so much," Marcus said as he rubbed me on the back.

"Hey, what are y'all over here doing?"

"Nothing, just setting the silverware out. What's up, P?"

"I was just coming to let you know that I'm taking Kiki to do her fitting on Friday at the bridal shop. The lady called me yesterday and left a voicemail, but I forgot to tell you."

"Ok, that's cool. I have to be there on Friday too. I guess we can all just ride together."

"Yeah, that's fine. Have you picked out your dress yet?"

"No, not yet. I haven't had a chance to drop by the boutique and get fitted. The only day I'm off is Friday."

"Ugh P, you know we're on a deadline, like damn; why you always wait until the last minute to do shit! You know Egypt is gonna flip out when she finds out."

"Egypt will be okay. She won't find out unless you go running your mouth to her."

I was just about to respond back to Paris when l I looked up and saw my brother coming through the door. I could spot him anywhere.

"Jashan! Oh my God, you finally made it!" I yelled in excitement as I ran over and hugged him. He'd gotten so tall over the years. I had to get on my tiptoes to reach him. He looked like a giant standing over me.

"Ari! I've missed you so much. I can't believe it's really you!" Jashan responded in a thick New Jersey accent.

"Awww, look at you! Got all tall on me and your voice is so deep." My little Jashan is all grown up."

"Yep. I'll be 21 next month."

"Dang, boy! You better be behaving yourself up there. I know how it is in Camden. You can get caught up, real fast."

"I am, sis; I'm doing well. Actually, I'm thinking about moving down here and playing college ball for Florida State. I got recruited a few months ago. Mikey is the one y'all better be worried about."

"Ah! Yes! Go ahead, baby brother. I'm so proud of you. Why didn't you tell me over the phone? I'll have a little talk with Mikey when he gets here. He thinks that because Grandma is old that he can do whatever he wants to do. He's not grown yet. He's only 17 years old."

"I know, sis. I've been trying to talk to him, but he's not trying to hear anything that anybody has to say. Plus, I wanted it to be a surprise," Jashan said.

"Well, he's gonna listen to me. I'll make his little ass move right down here when you come if I have to. Watch me."

"Yeah, good luck with that," Jashan laughed.

"What's all the commotion about over here? Y'all act like its—oh my God, Jashan, but it can't be!" Egypt said as she walked over to Jashan and stared up at him.

"Yes E, it's really him."

"Hey, Egypt. Long time, no see," Jashan said as he leaned down and hugged her.

"Ari, what in the world is going on?"

'I wanted to surprise you, E. I thought this would be the best wedding present ever."

"But how? I mean, how did all this happen?"

"Well, I found them on Facebook and we've been talking and texting every day for the past couple of months. I was gonna tell you soon, but I know you like surprises."

"So where's Mikey?"

"He should be here soon."

"Wow, this is just wonderful. I can't believe how much you've grown."

"Yeah, girl. And how about he's been recruited to Florida State."

"Say what? Get out of here. I'm so happy for you. Way to go!"

"Thanks, you guys."

"Look at him trying to sound all proper and shit," Egypt Joked.

The dinner went well and for the rest of the night, we all sat around and caught up on old times. Overall, I think everyone had a good time. Kiki and I stayed over after everyone left to help clean up. Jashan went to my house to take a shower and get some rest after all the riding he had done to get here. Mikey's flight was delayed, so he wasn't going to be here until tomorrow afternoon. Paris left early because she wasn't feeling too good. I wish she could have stayed and saw Jashan.

Egypt, Kiki, and I listened to music and played around while we cleaned up. There was so much food left over. I took some home with me, and it was still enough for about three more families to eat off of. Kiki and I finally left Egypt's around 5:00 a.m. When we got home, we were both too beat to even take a hot shower. I peeped my head inside the downstairs guest room and saw that Jashan was knocked out. I shut the door back and went upstairs to my room, kicked my shoes off, and laid down in the bed—fully dressed. Another drama-free night, just the way I liked it.

CHAPTER 33

EGYPT

"Hey Ari, what are you up to?"

"Nothing, what's up?"

"Shit! I was just calling to see if you and Marcus want to go out with me and Rodney this weekend?"

"Yeah, I guess he'll be down to go. Did I tell you I had that nigga screaming I love you while he was up in the pussy?"

"You so damn nasty, Ari; but you know he's just running game."

"You don't know; why is it hard to believe he loves me?" Ari asked.

"I wasn't saying it like that, Ari, and you know it. So don't be turning my words around. I could care less about y'alls dysfunctional ass relationship anyway. I was just saying."

"Hush E, dang. I was just playing with you, lighten up! Anyway girl, I love Kiki's dress. It fit her so nicely. She looks like a little princess. I hate to see my baby growing up on me," Ari said into the speakerphone.

"Aww yes, she looked too cute. We've definitely got to make sure we take pictures before the wedding is over."

"Yes, I was thinking the same thing; matter of fact, who are you getting to be the photographer?"

"I haven't decided yet. I've been checking online, but I still haven't found anyone local with a reasonable enough price. I'm not trying to pay a whole lot for pictures when it's a million other things that have to be paid for as well."

"Oh okay, I've been looking too. Just keep me informed. I've got to go, girl. I'm at work running my mouth and I got customers waiting on me," Ari whispered.

"Bye, girl; call me when you get off. Why you ain't say you were at work?" I laughed as I ended the call.

I sat in my office and counted the money from today's sales. With the hair appointments and profits from the new nail station, sales had really taken off. It was only Wednesday, but we made more in these past three days than we usually made on the weekend. That was our busiest time. I looked over at my phone when I heard it vibrate, indicating someone either called or texted. I picked it up and read the text across the screen

"YO, COME TO THE HOUSE AFTER WORK, BAE. I MISS U!!" with two smiley face emojis.

I replied back: "OKAY BE THERE SOON," with four hearts, one smiley face, and a diamond ring.

I put the phone back on my desk while I finished putting the money into the bank bag, so it could deposit it on my way to Rodney's. I walked over to each workstation and prepared everything for the next morning, just in case it got busy, like today. I didn't know who these girls were trying to impress with these new hair dos, but customers had been pouring in here like crazy. I walked out of the shop, but it suddenly started raining. I quickly double checked the locks before I took off running to my car, which was parked across the street in the parking garage.

"Woooh," I said, sitting down in the car. It felt good to finally sit down. I leaned my head back against the headrest and enjoyed the cool air that blew through the vents. It had been a long day, and all I wanted was to do was go to Rodney's house and take a long hot bubble bath. Knowing him, he already had it waiting for me. He always did when he knew I was coming straight over from work. When I pulled into Rodney's driveway, the first thing I noticed was another car already parked in my parking space. I looked the car up and down as I slowly pulled up behind it and cut my engine off. I hopped out and noticed it had a paper tag on it.

Hmm, I wonder who that could be, I thought as I walked up to it and peeped through the windows. It was filthy inside; old restaurant plates and cups were thrown all over the backseat. The seats were so stained up. It looked like it belonged in a junkyard. What kind of game was Rodney playing?

"Dang, he could have told me he already had company," I mumbled, as I walked up to the front door and knocked. After the third try, I reached in my purse and pulled out the key that Rodney had given me for emergencies. As soon as the door flew open, the smell of weed was heavy in the air. It hit my nose hard. The radio was blasting, but I could still hear laughing coming from upstairs. I crept up the stairs slowly, making sure not to make any noise. When I got in front of Rodney's room door, I paused because I heard moaning sounds.

"Oh hell no!" I yelled as I burst through the door ready for whatever, or so I thought. The door swung open and I just froze right there in the doorway. I was in shock as I watched the girl ride Rodney from the back. She was working her body while her small breasts bounced up and down in Rodney's hand. When our eyes connected, she just looked up at me and smiled. It was the most devious smile I had ever seen in my life. I tried my best to fight back the tears that burned my eyes. I felt like my heart was broken into a million pieces. The sight of the woman's sneaky ass smile set off something inside of me. Out of nowhere, I just pounced on the bed like a cat and started punching the girl in the face. Rodney jumped up, cussing and confused at what was happening at first.

"Oh shit! E! What the fuck? Yo, chill out!" Rodney yelled as he grabbed my arms and tried to pull me off of the girl.

"Get your fuckin' hands off me! How could you, Rodney?" I

shouted as I hit him over and over in the chest.

"I'm sorry, bae! Fuck! I didn't know you was coming over! Shit!"

"You want to cheat on me with some trashy looking bitch! How you ain't know when your dumb ass text me and told me to come over? What kinda shit you on, nigga? Matter of fact, you have can ya little hoe! It's over!" I yelled as I threw the engagement ring in his face and ran downstairs. Rodney grabbed his boxers and followed behind me, but he was too late. By the time he got to the front door, I was already speeding out the driveway.

CHAPTER 34

EGYPT

I cried the whole way home. When I pulled up to my house, I didn't even bother parking in the garage. I pulled in my driveway, hopped out my car, and ran inside. I locked the door behind me and ran upstairs. All I wanted was to be alone. I sat down on my bed and cried hard as hell as I looked through my phone at the pictures of me and Rodney. We looked so happy together. How could he just mess it up for some low life ass chick with a beat up ass car? *I know that bitch ass can't be clean just by looking at how she kept her car,* I thought as I hit ignore on the incoming call from Rodney.

He had called over 80 times in the last hour. I was not trying to hear any of his lies right now. I had been around long enough to know bullshit when I saw it. I thought Rodney had grown up by now, but I guess that he was still on that same little boy ass shit.

"Like damn, why ask someone to marry you if you're still gonna go around fucking random chicks?" I said aloud as I poured the last of the Moët in my wine glass. I shook the bottle a few times, trying to get every last drop out. It was only half a glass, so I got up and went downstairs to throw the empty bottle away and get a new one out the fridge. All of the lights were out except for the lamp in the hallway. Even though the kitchen was dark, I thought I saw someone standing in the corner. I thought my eyes were playing tricks on me at first, or that maybe I had too much wine for tonight. I reached for the light switch, but I was hit by a blow to the back of my head. I fell to the floor, kicking and screaming.

"Aaaaaahhh! Who's there? What do you want?" I screamed. I couldn't make out who it was or what they were doing. All I could feel was the pain in the back of my head. It felt like I was about to pass out.

"Yeah, bitch. You thought you were just gonna up and leave a nigga just like that? Huh? I got something for your hoe ass. You in here crying over a pussy ass nigga and I'm in New Jersey tearing the fucking hood up looking for your ass for 11 fucking years!" the intruder said as he dragged me back into the living room by my shirt. He stood over me as I looked up into his face.

"So you still confused, bitch? Now do you know who the fuck I am?"

"Oh my God!" My heart felt like it was about to jump out of my chest. I couldn't catch my breath.

"No baby, it's not God. It's the one and only."

"Peanut," I whispered. I backed up until my back was against the couch and I couldn't go any further.

"Damn right baby, in the mother fuckin flesh. Now tell Daddy you missed him! I damn sho' missed your ass," Peanut said as he leaned down and kissed me on the lips.

"Ew! Stop! Get the fuck away from me!" I yelled as I swung and connected my fist with the side of Peanut's face.

"Oh you trying to be tough, huh? You want to fight back now? I'll remind you what fighting back gets your ass. Yeah, you've been gone too long. It's time to remind you who the fuck Peanut is. I see you've forgotten!" he yelled, slapping me across the face and making blood squirt everywhere.

"Leave me alone! How did you even find me?" I screamed, as I got up off the floor and ran toward the front door. My hand touched the doorknob, but Peanut ran up behind me and punched me two times in the back of the head. The lick was so hard that I stumbled face-first into the small wooden table that sat by the front entrance. I looked over and saw my phone light up on the floor. I quickly picked it up and saw that it was Rodney calling. I missed the call and as soon as I tried to call him back, all I got was his voicemail.

"Aaaaaahhh! Help, Rodney help!" I yelled into the phone.

"Shut the fuck up, bitch! You over here crying over a nigga that don't want your stupid ass. You're so busy calling that nigga, but he laying up getting some of that bomb ass Spanish pussy, huh? Gimme that damn phone, bitch! You ain't calling no damn body. No one can save you this time," Peanut said as he snatched the phone out my hand and threw it into the wall, breaking it into tiny pieces.

"Leave me alone Peanut! Why don't you just move on? I don't want to be with you anymore."

"Oh, you want to be left alone, huh? Okay, I'll show your punk ass how it felt to be left alone. It's not over until I say it's over, bitch!" Peanut yelled as he grabbed a handful of my hair and slammed my face into the floor.

"Ah! No! Peanut, please don't do this! I'm sorry," I pleaded.

"Nah, you're not sorry yet, but you're gonna be! You just gonna say fuck me huh, just run your ass off without even saying a word? Trust me, I've got something for my lying ass cousin Ari too. Y'all bitches thought it was over, huh?" he said, slamming my face into the floor again.

I begged over and over for Peanut to stop beating me, but it just made him hit me even harder. He beat me until I was no longer moving. Everything around me went black and I couldn't feel any more pain.

CHAPTER 35

RODNEY

"Yo, get the fuck out!"

"What? Why are you acting all funny and shit all of a sudden?" Marisol questioned.

"Look, you heard what the fuck I said! Put your fucking clothes on and get the hell out."

"Whatever nigga, I don't have time for your bullshit. You weren't acting like this all before, but you want to change up now that your little bitch caught your ass."

"Say what?"

"You heard me. Everything was all good when you were coming to my hotel room all week. You were fucking me whenever you wanted it. Matter of fact, the same hotel room that you're paying the bill for. I bet your little bitch wouldn't like that too much, huh?"

"Kill all that. Yeah, you're right. I fucked your little hoe ass because you kept begging for the dick. You threw it at me, so why not take it? You knew what it was. As a matter of fact, you're screaming about my girl but I don't recall ever mentioning her to you. I damn sure didn't text her and tell her to come over here. So why the fuck would she say I did? Huh? I knew your ass was up to no good!" I yelled, as I walked up and stood in Marisol's face.

"Fuck you and that bitch! She don't deserve you anyway! You're mine, and you'll always be mine."

"Marisol, don't play with me! I'll break your fuckin' neck! Your dirty ass set me up? I should have never trusted your ass again. Damn, why the fuck did I bring your stanking ass to my crib in the first place? I should have known something was up when your ass kept begging to come through. Fuck! Fuck! I should have just told E the truth after we got the blood test results back, but no. I had to take my dumb ass up to your room instead. What was I thinking?"

"Yep, nigga, I sure did! Trater con el! You thought you were just going to fuck me whenever you wanted to and then just run off and marry Miss Project bitch! So I guess your son and I are just supposed to watch y'all walk away into the sunset? Huh? I don't think so, hijo de puta! Why can't you be happy with me again? Huh? Me, you, and Jaquan can be a family. Just like we always talked about."

"Man, kill all that sad shit that you're trying to sell. You fucked that up, so blame yourself! I hope you didn't think I was going to be with your ass after all the shit you've done to me. A nigga tried to fuck with your ass on a friend level, but you can't understand that. You want to go behind my back and do sneaky shit! Yo ass just can't be trusted at all."

"Okay, so what about Jaquan? What are we supposed to do?"

"My son has nothing to do with what your grimy ass did. Trust me, my son will be well taken care of. I don't have to be with you in order to take care of my seed. Now, get your little scheming ass out my crib before you make me put my hands on you. I'm trying not to hurt your stupid ass. Plus, I need to go check on my ol' lady and see if I can mend what your dumb ass tried to sabotage."

"Yeah, good luck with that!" Marisol said, looking down at her phone.

"Shut the fuck up. Why are you still here? Bye! You know the way out," I said, pointing toward the door.

"Whatever nigga, you're saying all this now, but I promise you before it's all said and done, you are going to be begging me. You'll eat those same words, I PROMISE YOU THAT!!" Marisol said as she walked down the stairs and then out of the front door.

"Yeah, yeah! Ain't nobody trying to hear all that. I'll holla at your ass in court!" I yelled as I stood in the doorway and watched her tail lights disappear out of the driveway. I pulled my phone out of my pocket and tried to call Egypt again, but I still got no answer. *Fuck it, I'm going over there.*

I jumped on my motorcycle and headed to Egypt's house. Twenty minutes later, I pulled into Egypt's driveway and parked my motorcycle behind her car. I knocked on the front door a few times, but she didn't answer. I could hear the radio on, so I knew she was in there. She was probably crying her eyes out. Damn, I never meant to hurt her like this, especially not with Marisol of all people. I messed up this time. Since Egypt wouldn't answer the door, I figured I would go next door to Paris' house and see if she was over there.

"Paris! Paris! Yo Paris!"

"Rodney? Is that you?" Paris asked, peeping out the side window by her front door. She hit the switch for the porch light before she opened it.

"Yeah, open the door. I need to talk to you."

"Boy, it's after midnight. What's going on? You're beating on my door like you're the police," Paris said, opening the door.

"My bad, sis. I'm sorry to come over this late, but I was trying to see if E was over here. Have you seen her?"

"Nah, she not over here. She wasn't home?" Paris said in a concerned tone.

"I don't think so. Her car is parked out front, but she's not answering. She probably is in there listening to me knock," I said.

"What in the world? What's going on with y'all? Maybe she is asleep. I mean, it's going on one in the morning." Paris said sarcastically, hoping I got the hint to leave.

"Nah, I don't think so because the radio is blasting. We had a little disagreement earlier and she got mad. I've been trying to call her ever since she left my crib, but she ain't answering."

"Mm hmm, I don't know what to say about y'all. Hold on, let me try to call her and see if she picks up for me. You know how stubborn Egypt is." Paris dialed her number. "She didn't answer," Paris replied as she walked back into the front room holding her phone up to show me she had really made the call.

"See, now I know damn well that if she were still awake then she would have answered the phone for you. No matter what. I'm telling you something just doesn't seem right. I know you've got a key. Come on, let's go make sure she's okay, and then I'll leave you alone."

Paris didn't answer at first; she just became quiet. I could tell she was thinking about what I had just said. She knew that I was right. No matter what Egypt was doing, she would have stopped to answer whenever Paris called, even if she was in a bad mood.

"Okay, let's walk over there, hold on," Paris finally said. About five minutes later, she came running downstairs with her sweat pants and sneakers on.

"Dang sis, what took you so long, and why are you dressed like you're about to go whoop some ass?"

"Cause, you never know," Paris said, walking to the front

door.

When we got to Egypt's house, I could hear the radio blasting inside. Paris knocked on the door a few times, but Egypt still didn't answer. I looked around and nothing seemed out of the ordinary. Knowing Egypt, she in one of her little moods and just didn't want to be bothered.

"Yo, just use your key. I told you that she wasn't going to answer."

"Shh, stop making all that noise. What are you trying to do? Wake up the whole neighborhood? Dang, hold on, I'm trying to get it in. I can't see a tiny hole on this dark ass porch! You ain't no help!"

When she finally got the door unlocked, we walked inside. Broken glass was everywhere. Paris ran upstairs to Egypt's bedroom while I checked around downstairs. Pictures and tables were broken in the front room. It looked like someone was fighting. I know I didn't make her so mad to destroy everything she worked so hard to get. Paris came running downstairs yelling Egypt's name.

"E, it's your sister! Where are you? Are you okay?" she called out. "I don't see her anywhere. So what happened? Why did she get mad at you anyway?

"Just a little misunderstanding," I lied.

"Um huh, misunderstanding my ass! You better not have hurt my fuckin' sister, Rodney!"

"Girl, ain't nobody did shit to your sister. Why the hell would I come knocking on your door if I had done something to her, huh?" Rodney asked

"I don't know. All of this shit is just so strange. Egypt wouldn't just leave without telling me. Her car is parked out front."

"What's strange?"

"Oh my God. You scared the shit out of me!" Paris yelled as we both looked behind us and found Ari standing in the doorway.

"I saw all the lights on and the front door was wide open, so I came over to see what was going on," Ari said.

"Have you seen Egypt?"

"No, I talked to her earlier today when I was at work, but that's it. Why, what's going on, and why is glass all over the place?"

"I don't know. Rodney showed up at my house about 30 minutes ago looking for her because she wouldn't answer the door. Then when we get over here, I used my spare key to check the house and she's nowhere to be found. I don't know what happened. Glass is everywhere."

"What? Where the hell could she have gone this time of night and without her car? You know damn well E ain't walking anywhere," Ari said.

"Exactly, I have no idea where she could be."

I was quiet as I sat on the couch in Egypt's living room. I was staring at my phone while Ari and Paris talked in the hallway. I noticed a little envelope in the corner of the screen, indicating I had a voicemail. I decided to check it, hoping it wasn't Marisol cursing and screaming. I put the phone to my ear so that I could hear the message better. As soon as it started to play, my eyes grew. I ran into the hallway where Paris and Ari were standing.

"Oh shit! Y'all listen to this," I said, putting my phone on speaker.

"Aaaaaah! Nooo please stop! Rodney help ple—"

Ari and Paris just stood there frozen in one spot. The sound of Egypt begging and pleading for her attacker to stop broke all three of our hearts. Her voice echoed over and over in my head. Ari broke down in tears and Paris tried to console her the best that she could. They both fell to the floor on their knees, crying and praying to God that Egypt was okay. I couldn't take hearing them plead to God for Egypt's life. I felt like I failed her as a man. I was supposed to be her protector and once again, I allowed her to get hurt. Someone had to pay for this. I kneeled down on the floor and put my arms around both of their shoulders.

"Aye, y'all got to be strong for her right now. I know we're all thinking the worst, but we got to stay positive. We can't assume the worst just yet. I know my baby and she's a fighter. I know she fought whoever it was. That's why she tried to call me for help," I whispered to Ari and Paris as I tried hard to hold back my own tears.

"Come on, I need y'all. We've got to pull it together. I need for one of y'all to call the police department and ask for Detective Samuels. Tell him you're my sister and explain the situation. He'll know what to do. When he gets here, let him hear the voicemail. I just forwarded it to you, P. I need y'all on that ASAP! We don't have time to play around right now."

"Okay, but where are you going?" Paris asked.

"I got some shit to handle. I won't rest until my baby is back in my arms. Everybody's gonna pay. I don't give a damn who they are, young or old! Every mother fuckin body is a target right now. I tried to be good. You know, do the right thing. Live my life on the straight and narrow, but motherfuckas want to see the real Rodney. They're not gonna be satisfied until I bring him back out. Well, I'm back!"

"Nah bruh, come on now. Don't do any dumb shit and get locked back up. You've got too much to lose. You're about to be married in a few weeks, and you know Egypt will have a fit if you're not there," Paris said.

"How can I get married when my fuckin' bride is nowhere to be found?" I said in a calm voice as I kissed her on the forehead and walked out the door. Paris knew I was about to make Miami feel my wrath, and there wasn't a soul that could stop me.

I went home and switched from the motorcycle to my Tahoe. I drove around for a few hours drinking and trying to wrap my mind around everything. After about two hours of searching every hood in Miami that I could think of, I pulled into a Wendy's parking lot and just sat in the truck. The tears rolled down my face as I banged my fist onto the steering wheel. It'd been a long time since anything made me shed a tear. I cursed myself for being so stupid.

Damn! I tried to do right! I should have never fucked with that bitch again. Why didn't I just make Egypt's stubborn ass move in with me? I told her it wasn't safe being in that big ass house all alone, but no. She always had to have shit her way. Now look, if I would have been with her instead of Marisol, none of this shit would have happened! I felt like my whole life was over. Every time I did some fuck shit, something bad happened. Deep down, something was telling me Marisol's snake ass was behind this. It had her name written all over it. I didn't know, but my next stop was Richmond, VA.

Whoever crossed me was gonna pay dearly. I wasn't the one

you wanted to fuck with. Marisol better pray to God that she had nothing to do with this because if she did, baby momma or not, her ass was dying right alongside the mother fuckas that helped her. I knew she couldn't do it by herself. Damn! Just when a thug found true love. I turned the liquor bottle up and pulled out of the parking lot, then headed to the interstate with only one thing on my mind. Egypt.

TO BE CONTINUED

Like me on Facebook at

Authoressjazminewrightfanpage@facebook.com

Follow me on Twitter at

Authoressjazminewright@twitter.com

CPSIA information can be obtained at www.ICGtesting.com
Printed in the USA
LVOW10s1340221016

509751LV00017B/963/P